W9-BPK-365

PEDEN
Peden, Peggy O'Neal,
Gone missin' /

GONE MISSIN'

GONE MISSIN'

Peggy O'Neal Peden

SEVERN HOUSE

First world edition published in Great Britain in 2021 and the USA in 2022
by Severn House, an imprint of Canongate Books Ltd,
14 High Street, Edinburgh EH1 1TE.

Trade paperback edition first published in Great Britain and the USA in 2022
by Severn House, an imprint of Canongate Books Ltd.

severnhouse.com

British Library Cataloguing-in-Publication Data
A CIP catalogue record for this title is available from the British Library.

ISBN-13: 978-0-7278-5084-3 (cased)
ISBN-13: 978-1-4483-0635-0 (trade paper)
ISBN-13: 978-1-4483-0634-3 (e-book)

All Severn House titles are printed on acid-free paper.

Typeset by Palimpsest Book Production Ltd.,
Falkirk, Stirlingshire, Scotland.
Printed and bound in Great Britain by
TJ Books, Padstow, Cornwall.

Dedicated to Mom and Dad, to Mark and Mike, to David.

And to the nurses, doctors, hospital staff, grocery workers, truck drivers, maintenance workers, lab technicians and waiters who have worked to take care of us and keep us fed.

In memory of Dr Constance Fulmer.

ONE

Was it a dream
When we danced that night?
Was it a dream?
Part of the plan or just a chance?
And where are you now?
Where are you now?

Was it a dream
When you held me so tight?
Was it a dream?
Part of the plan or just being young in the night?
And where are you now?
Where are you now?

Snowflakes on your hair
Moonlight in your eyes
Magic in the air
Forever in your sighs

Stick Anderson

The night might have been ordered by the Decorations Committee, and if anyone in Nashville had the power to order the weather, these women did. They were the power behind the power in the downtown skyscrapers: the wives of the lawyers, the bankers and brokers and developers, a few distinguished physicians. Their names and their husbands' names had been calling the shots in this town for a hundred years, some longer than that. So, on a crisply cold night, the Saturday after Thanksgiving, a night that seemed too clear and sharp for precipitation, the snow fell. Beautifully, gently, it fell like confectioner's sugar from a sieve, dusting the evergreens and the roofs, catching the light from streetlights and the twinkling lights in sidewalk trees, lightly touching the perfect hair of the beautiful women, laughing as they shrugged their politically incorrect but exquisite furs more closely around their faces and dashed into the Vanderbilt Plaza Hotel. No ice on West End to slow the schedule or make the orchestra late, no ugly slush to stain the hems of the debutantes' white gowns, just lovely, white snowflakes drifting, floating, turning the whole city into a magic snow globe background for one perfect evening for fifty young women making their debut in polite Nashville society.

It was, however, the twenty-first century. There were no statistics on how many of the twenty-ish young women in their requisite white gowns were actually virginal. The décolletage, the sequins, the slits and the beading suggested a sophistication that the ball's founders decades ago might not have approved. Watching their parents and friends beam and applaud as they were presented, though, escorted by young men, all handsome and strong in their unaccustomed tuxedos, how could one think them anything but perfect; full of promise and potential, bright and as attractive as good hairstylists and orthodontists could make them, ready to become the next generation of mothers and wives of power brokers, but now, maybe, power brokers themselves. Some things changed. Now, even the daughters could hope for a spot in Daddy's firm.

They hugged and waved, chattering from group to group, catching up with high school friends, everyone home from Auburn or Ole Miss, Virginia, Alabama or Sewanee, exclusive private colleges or even UT, a few from eastern schools, home for the holiday weekend. With the Tennessee–Vanderbilt game in Nashville this year, a few Vandy football players were escorts, although they came in a little late, their hair still damp from the rush to shower and change, cheered from a moral victory after leading UT more than once and ending with a score close enough to annoy University of Tennessee fans bent on a top bowl. There was more laughing than dancing. Montgomery Bell Academy–Brentwood Academy, Ensworth football games were replayed, and Harpeth Hall dances remembered.

At the tables around the dance floor were families and a few invited guests, catching up with friends with whom they shared a history if not everyday routine. Mixed in with the mothers and fathers and grandparents were younger couples, too young to have children in this parade but old enough to remember their own nights like this with nostalgia or irony, depending on how life had treated them.

Bitsy and Philip were there, of course. Bitsy was co-chair this year. It had been ten years or more since her own debut, and Philip had never seen this kind of spectacle until he had married her and moved to Nashville. But this was their world, and they both moved through it, laughing, hugging, Bitsy accepting congratulations on a beautiful ball with a gracious shrug, tossing her blonde hair. 'It plans itself,' she laughed, 'we've been doing it so long.'

Philip wouldn't allow that, though. 'She's been working herself to death,' he insisted. 'The kids could tell you the table arrangements and exactly what time the orchestra was to start. Nothing about this party is an accident.'

Anyone looking at the centerpieces and favors on the tables, the twinkling lights suspended from the ceiling in cloud-like acres of net, knew it was true. But Bitsy didn't betray a moment of stress. She could make self-deprecating jokes with the absolute confidence of a woman who knew all her friends would be jealously talking over this night for weeks. She could be gracious; she could be humble because it was all perfect. And that meant she was perfectly filling the role she had chosen. Her best friend Alice from Harpeth Hall might be a pediatrician, but Bitsy was the Deb Ball chair who could make even the weather cooperate. She might look a bit more mature than the girls in white gowns this year, but no less perfect. And Philip, too, handsome, shaking hands, clapping friends on the shoulder, laughing about golf games and the sweet spots of new drivers. They were a perfect couple, the fulfillment of tonight's promise, except, of course, that Philip hadn't been born in this world, hadn't been part of it until Bitsy brought him home, hadn't been to balls like this, probably hadn't thought they still existed until after he married Bitsy. But he certainly looked as if he had always belonged

here. And their two children, a girl and a boy, well, with
parents like Bitsy and Philip, how could they be anything but
beautiful?

TWO

Snowflakes on your hair
Moonlight in your eyes
Magic in the air
Forever in your sighs

Stick Anderson

I wasn't surprised to hear that Bitsy Carter had gone to
Mexico. It was just like Bitsy to pack up and head for
Zihuatanejo when Nashville went gray in February. I'm
Campbell Hale; I manage a travel agency in Nashville's
Hillsboro Village, and Bitsy had been a client of mine for
years. She traveled a lot, especially when the weather somewhere else in the world was better than it was in Nashville,
warmer, cooler, dryer. I was a little surprised, though, that
Bitsy had called in for her ticket and to make her travel plans
on a day when I was out of the office. We'd become friends
over the years. She knew my schedule, and usually she
was adamant about waiting for me, but Martha, another agent
in the office, told me she had called on Wednesday, my regular
day off. She had asked, Martha said, for the tickets to be
electronic and to be sent to her. That was a little unusual, too;
ordinarily she came by to pick up her tickets and travel documents, wanted everything printed out that could be. We would
catch up; sometimes we'd go to lunch. I assumed she was
busy or in a hurry.

It wasn't until the police came by a couple of weeks later
and started asking questions that I began to realize how really
odd it was. After two weeks, Bitsy's husband and parents had

reported her missing. They had been concerned from the beginning, but Bitsy had left a note saying that she needed to get away alone for a while. Philip said she'd been stressed. She had apparently decided suddenly and left within a day or so. No one could believe she'd leave the country without even calling. Bitsy traveled often, and it wasn't unusual for her to travel alone, but she also talked to her parents frequently. Philip said they'd had an argument, but not a serious one, Bitsy saying he left everything to her to manage, which he acknowledged was mostly true, that she needed a break, let him handle the kids and house for a few days. The dialogue sounded familiar to any married couple, but still it wasn't like her to leave without telling them where she would be. At the end of two weeks, they called the police. It wasn't like her to go two weeks without talking to them, no matter where she was.

Bitsy had, for the first time in ten years, also missed an annual lunch reunion with her best friends from high school. Most of them ran into each other often. Some of their kids were in the same schools; some of them went to the same churches, but this lunch date was sacred. The few who lived out-of-town came in. It was one of the first things entered on a new calendar. Missing it was not a casual thing. Four days before the lunch, the day before she had disappeared (they were calling it a disappearance now), Bitsy had called her friend Angie to tell her how much she was looking forward to getting together with them. Leaving like that and letting down people who were counting on her wasn't like Bitsy at all.

Bitsy was also having some remodeling done at her Belle Meade home. The contractors, a couple who were also clients of mine, had met with her the day she disappeared. They had apparently been the last ones to talk with her, and they were to start work the following morning. Bitsy had said she would expect them at seven. When they arrived at seven, Philip, just leaving for work, told them she would be away for a few days. Just go ahead with whatever Bitsy had said, he told them. They started ripping out the master bath as planned and figured she had wanted to take a pass on their mess.

Oddest of all was that Bitsy had missed Parents' Day at her daughter Rachel's kindergarten. Bitsy had grown up in Nashville's Belle Meade with a nanny who cared for her and, until she got her license and her own car – an Alpha Romeo Spider almost like mine – drove her to school and to go shopping and to parties. Not one to fix what wasn't broken, she had a nanny for her own children. Bitsy called her an au pair and said the children wouldn't know what to do without Maureen. But Bitsy rarely missed a ball game and had never missed Parents' Day.

We were incredibly busy when the police came in. Our busiest part of the year is from the second week in January until mid-May. Everyone is planning spring break and summer vacations. You can't hire enough full-time staff to work comfortably through those months and have half your people twiddling their thumbs from May through December. You try to hit a medium, survive through the winter and early spring and encourage staff vacations to be scheduled in the fall. We had all been working late for weeks.

So it was that kind of day when Detectives Davis and Anderson came in the front door. For a quick, foolishly optimistic moment I let myself think that Detective Davis might be coming by just to see me. We had met a few months earlier when he had been investigating a case. I was in the victim's house at the time of the murder. I had been wandering around where I had no right to be. I started out as a potential suspect and ended up with a concussion, a wrecked car and a – what? Friend? Acquaintance? Hard to say. We tended to get each other's bristles up, but we were becoming friends and occasionally had dinner or went to movies together. Either way, we wound up arguing before the evening was over.

I could tell when I looked more closely, though, that Sam, Detective Davis, was all business, and I wondered what I had done wrong.

'Campbell. We need to ask you a few questions, maybe talk to some of your staff, and' – he pulled a folded paper from his sport coat pocket – 'we have a subpoena for some records.'

All work stopped, and every head swiveled toward the

policemen. Fortunately, there were no clients in the room. 'Is this something we need to talk about in my office, Detective?'

'You can call me Sam.' He smiled. 'I'm not here to arrest you. Not this time, anyway. No, I know I'm interrupting you, but if it's OK with you, Campbell, I think it might be helpful to talk to everyone here.'

I looked around. 'OK, gang, no Miranda rights. I think we can beat this later if we have to.' I turned back to Sam and Detective Anderson, who was obviously enjoying the exchange. 'What's this about?'

Sam explained, occasionally referring to Detective Anderson for details. There had been no word from Bitsy in just over two weeks. Her husband and parents had called her hotel near Zihuatanejo several times, but there had never been an answer in her room. The hotel staff indicated that she had checked in, but no one there had seen her since. They sent someone to her room, but no one was there when they checked. Maids reported that after the first night, the bed in her room did not appear to have been slept in. No luggage was left in the room. It had been cleaned, according to the hotel's regulations, every morning, so few traces of any inhabitants were likely to remain.

'Do you think something's happened to her?' I asked.

'So far, we're treating it officially as a missing person, but the longer we wait, the colder the information gets, and the shadier it seems.'

I went to the back to get our file copy of the invoice. Sam followed me. He slumped into a chair while I began to search through files. Invoices are filed by the date the ticket was issued, not the date of travel, so that took a little figuring, but I knew it was on a Wednesday, since I was off, which helped.

Sam is tall, maybe six feet four, and he fills up a room. When he was seated, as he was now, his presence seemed to spread out, his arms and legs all angles and lines, too long to fit the chair. 'What can you tell me about this woman?' he asked.

I tried to tell him what I knew of Bitsy. I found myself talking about Bitsy pulling out her day planner to make sure she wouldn't miss a YMCA league soccer game or cupcake day at preschool. I told him how Bitsy didn't go places everybody else went, how she always seemed to be going full speed, rushing to meet life, making up for her sheltered existence in a driven reach to capture experience that was real and on the edge. It was hard to talk about Bitsy without mixing metaphors. 'Bitsy might be lying on a beach with waiters spritzing her with imported mineral water, but if she's sightseeing, it won't be from a tour bus. She'll be riding a mule or hiking or kayaking. When she goes, she goes all out.'

'Are you sure it was Mrs Carter who called that day? You'd know her voice?'

I told him that I would definitely have known her voice, but I hadn't talked to her. I didn't think Martha or anyone else in the office would know for sure that it was Bitsy over the phone.

'And you didn't talk to her when she picked up her ticket?'

I explained about Martha saying Bitsy had asked that the tickets be sent.

'And that was unusual?'

'For Bitsy.'

'Would she have had to sign for them? Would you have a FedEx tracking number, a delivery receipt or something like that?'

'No, the ticket was mailed Priority Mail. We do that since the airlines have started issuing electronic tickets. What you get isn't an actual ticket; it's a receipt showing that you have purchased an electronic ticket. If it's lost, it's no big deal; the information still exists. We could have emailed the receipt and confirmation, and she could have printed it out herself. People who book their own air and hotel reservations usually do. That's easier and easier all the time. So we can mail documents, even email them. There's no tracking number, no signature required. That's why you can book online and print off the paper you take to the airport. That piece of paper isn't an actual ticket. The ticket exists in the computer software, in the cloud or something. If you lose it, no big deal. You print out another one, and it works just as well. You can even confirm your ticket and print out your boarding pass from a machine at the airport.'

'So all we really know is that a woman called in saying she was Bitsy Carter.'

I looked at him, suddenly alert in his chair. 'You're right, but I don't see how that would matter. You can't board a plane now without photo identification that matches the ticket or receipt. For an international flight, she would have had to show her passport. The TSA isn't as strict on Mexico, especially going in this direction, as on, say, Europe or the Middle East, but still it's not like the old days. People used to be able to slide by with initials instead of first names, things like that, but not anymore.'

Sam dropped his head into his hands. 'I just met with her family. Mr Thompson, her father, offered to call the mayor, the governor and the president if I needed any resources. And he can really do that. He can get through to those people. I could handle that, but her little boy, Thompson, six years old, followed me to the door and asked me to bring his mommy home. I don't think I'm going to like this.'

I found the invoice, the pink copy of a four-part form. Clients get the white copy; the ticketing agent keeps the pale yellow one, and the goldenrod copy is thrown away after accounting processing. The pink one is kept on file for three years. 'Is this all you need?'

'I don't know. How can I find out if she actually flew on this reservation?'

'We don't have any way of tracking that. You'd have to go to the airline, and it probably won't be easy. I can try to find out, but you'll probably need another subpoena for anything you could use as evidence. This is the airline's record locator' – I pointed to a six-digit combination letter and number code and then to a longer number – 'and this is the actual ticket number. You'll need those when you talk to the airline people.'

'Look, Campbell, I'm going to go back out front and talk to everybody, but after we leave, you are all going to be talking about this the rest of the day, probably for days. I'm not looking for evidence now; I'm looking for leads, information, ideas, anything. Just remember what you all say. That's when things will come to you, all of you, when you're talking about this with each other. OK?'

'Sure. Of course.'

We went back to the front where Detective Anderson was taking a statement from Martha. Sam listened, asking again if Martha knew if the woman who had called was actually Bitsy Carter.

'I wouldn't know her voice. She said, "This is Bitsy Carter" and I took her word for it. I recognize some people's voices, mostly my regular clients, occasionally somebody who has an unusual or distinctive voice. Like, you know, Campbell, that songwriter who's British, and everybody loves his voice, used to write with Emmylou Harris, but I know hardly anybody by voice who's not a regular of mine. I wouldn't even remember having talked to her except that she's Campbell's client. Usually she waits to talk to Campbell, insists on it even. I made a point of telling Campbell because I didn't want her to think I was trying to get the commission.'

I explained to Sam that, in addition to our salaries, each of us makes a small percentage commission on each ticket or trip we book. It adds up, but the amount on any individual sale isn't enough to get upset about. We do, however, try to be considerate of each other when regular clients call in. What goes around comes around. Unlike many clients, Bitsy knew about our commission arrangement, but her asking for me was more a matter of personal loyalty, that and that I knew what she liked and how she liked it. I made travel easy for Bitsy. Bitsy liked to do business with people who made life easy for her.

Martha explained to Sam that she had not had to ask for a credit card number, frequent flier number, address or other information that few people but Bitsy could have supplied, because all of that was in a computerized profile.

'There's a hotel reservation confirmation on this invoice,' Sam said to Martha. 'Does that mean you made the hotel reservation, too?'

'Yeah. She said she wanted to go to stay at a spa. There's a great one there near Ixtapa and Zihuatanejo. It's kind of away from things, but she said that was fine. She said somebody had told her about this one, but she was kind of vague. She wanted to get away from things.'

'What kind of things? Did she say? Did she offer any more information? Any side remarks about what she wanted to get away from?'

'I don't think so.' Martha shrugged. 'Not that I remember anyway.'

'How would she have gotten from the airport to the hotel? Did she rent a car?'

'No, at least, I didn't book her one. The spa has a shuttle, a limo, and, when I made her reservation, I gave them her flight times so they would know when to pick her up. It's pretty far out.'

'Far out?'

'Far from the airport, far out of town. And the idea of the spa is that you're totally spoiled, totally taken care of. A lot of people who go to spas like that are older women, and they don't want to have to figure out how to get somewhere on their own.'

'So she wouldn't have been likely to be wandering around Mexico on her own? As far as you know, she didn't have her own transportation?'

'As far as I know.'

Sam asked for any information we had on the spa. I made photocopies from our hotel guide as well as a couple of other hotel rating surveys. They gave him phone and fax numbers, the current manager's name, number and types of rooms, rates, amenities, services and photographs, more than he could access online. The property was also listed in an only slightly out-of-date guidebook to spas in North America. I made a photocopy of the invoice Sam was taking with him to replace in our file, and he and Detective Anderson left.

Sam was right. We didn't do much else that afternoon except talk about Bitsy and what might have happened to her. We hadn't seen her husband Philip as much as we had Bitsy, but he had always been polite, friendly, courteous when any of us had had any contact with him.

Martha was suspicious. 'It's always the husband. Besides,

he's too nice, too good-looking.' Philip was sun-bleached blond, with skin that always seemed tan from golf or skiing. Martha was right. He was too good-looking, but in a boy-next-door kind of way, not too pretty-boy.

'That doesn't make him a prime suspect for kidnapping or murder,' Lee insisted. He was the only man in the office and felt the burden of representing his gender in office discussions. 'He's a nice guy? Oh, yeah, he must be a killer. There's got to be something wrong with a man who's nice.'

Martha was unconvinced. Anna suspected a lover. Anna had an unhappy marriage she would do nothing about, and she was always inventing illicit love affairs for clients. We thought it was projection.

Lee also mentioned recent news reports about tourists in Mexico being victims of a variety of crimes from picked pockets to murder. And there were always drug traffickers. None of our clients had had any trouble in Mexico, so we had tended to discount the news stories as rating's month sensationalism, but now we wondered. Late that afternoon, one of the local television stations called to ask for comments or an interview. I was relieved to be able to say that would violate client confidentiality. I declined.

THREE

Was it a dream
When you danced with me?
Was it a dream?
Part of God's plan or just a chance?
And where are you now?
Where are you now?

couldn't let go of Bitsy's disappearance, and I turned the radio off as I drove home. The disc jockey was annoying, or maybe the problem was me. I wanted answers, and there was too little information. Just speculation, but the family was prominent enough that the story was on the radio news, and the non-news was making me mad. It was one of those rare but glorious winter afternoons in Nashville, though. The temperature was just over sixty, and there wasn't a cloud in the sky. I opened the sunroof and let the wind blow through the car and my mind. I was driving a leased white Camry because my Spider, the beautiful, red 1966 Alfa Romeo Spider 1600 I had driven since college, the car my parents had given me, that my dad had taught me to nurture and take care of, the reason I'd first gotten to know Bitsy, had been demolished a few months back. It was being rebuilt, but, since I didn't have a fortune and the insurance company had declared it a total loss, and because parts for a '66 Spider are hard to find, it was taking a long time. The sun was bright and low, but it was mostly at my back as I headed east on 440 toward Donelson and home. Some of the forsythia in the median was being fooled into thinking it was time to bloom. The stop-and-slow traffic gave me plenty of time to think, but all I had were questions. Would Bitsy have left without contacting anyone? Had something happened to her in Mexico?

I headed east on I-40 and took the Briley Parkway exit north. Just past Opry Mills I exited on Music Valley Drive. I really needed a birthday gift for one of my nephews. I was thinking of something for camping, and I knew I could find it at the Bass Pro Shop in Opry Mills, but I couldn't bring myself to take the exit into the shopping center. I wasn't in the mood for shopping. The Opry Mills exit was not designed for easy access to the Mall. It was built to control traffic into the old Opryland Amusement Park. It was built to manage traffic, slow it down. Nashville has better and better shopping all the time, great stores that sell things I used to have to order from catalogs, but now there's more traffic, more potholes, more hassle.

I yearn for the old days when you could park twenty feet from the door of the Donelson Castner-Knott store on your way home from church, pick up a wedding shower gift, leave it with someone in Customer Service that you knew at least enough to nod to, and pick it up wrapped a couple of hours later after dinner or a Sunday afternoon nap as you were on your way back to the shower. I have realized lately that I am somewhat resistant to change. I may not be the only one, though. Castner-Knott, once one of Nashville's two leading department stores, doesn't exist anymore. There are clubs, though, of former employees who still get together to reminisce. Maybe I'm not alone.

It's true that Bitsy and I come from different worlds. Our friendship seemed unlikely. Sometimes I found it hard to believe that Bitsy's world still existed. I thought it had gone the way of the industrial robber barons, riding west on the rails they built to linger in Southern California before vanishing forever into the sea. There are still, though, pockets of such privilege and protection, and Nashville's Belle Meade is one of them. Nashville is definitely Music City, but there's much more here than country music. There is still a season in Belle Meade complete with debutante balls, and that was Bitsy's world. Bitsy had, in fact, been on the committee for one of the major deb balls just a few months before, and she had invited me to see for myself how the other two percent lived. It was Thanksgiving weekend, and I had loved it. Every parent was proud; every girl was a princess, the demureness of each pure white gown belied by all-out competition in style, cut and beading. By the time dinner was over, though, and the presentation and the dancing, I was reminded of the crosses princesses must bear. My feet hurt.

I had grown up in a small town with one traffic light and no deb balls. It wasn't that I had grown up on the other side of the tracks; we didn't even have tracks in my hometown. Unlikely as it might seem, Bitsy and I had become friends of a sort. We liked each other. Bitsy was privileged, but she had a depth and intelligence that her name belied. How could I not like and respect someone who had the good judgment to like and respect me?

We had met in the grimy, miniscule waiting room of an auto repair place near the fairgrounds. You wouldn't stop there if you didn't know that Charlie, the mastermind behind AAAAuto, had the best hands in town when it came to imported sports cars. While Bitsy also had other vehicles in the garage to choose from, the Spider was her favorite. She wouldn't let anybody touch it except Charlie, and it was pampered as a Spider must be, regular oil changes and tune-ups, hand-wax detailing. Bitsy's Spider was almost like mine, a few years newer, but shiny red and loved as much as mine. She'd had hers since high school; I'd had mine since college. If that wasn't a bond, what was? So it bothered me to think that something might have happened to her.

On Music Valley, I drove past the music theaters, outlet stores and timeshare vacation rentals until the road ended at the Cumberland River. I turned right, parallel to the river, on my narrow little road with its No Tourist Attractions Beyond This Point sign. There are just a few houses back here, clinging to the bluff above the river as the tourism industry keeps pushing, hungrily reaching for land and river views. My house hides under trees and behind shrubbery that really should be pruned back. Grass doesn't grow well in all that shade, but I have a soft moss lawn with lichen and ivy blurring the lines between the limestone bluff and the matching stone house. I can't grow much, but I can grow some beautiful shade-loving impatiens. And I have great neighbors: the Morgans next door are too far away to be up in my business, but close enough to see if my lights are on and hear if I holler for help. I parked on the river gravel drive and noticed that my early bulbs were coming up. I'd be lucky to see those hyacinths bloom. More than likely the next cold snap would freeze their optimistic little buds off.

Inside I opened all the shutters wide. At that time of year, it was already almost dark, but the lights from the *General Jackson* riverboat reflected off the surface of the water when it passed. Out back, beyond the flagstone patio, I could see the river, and, as always, it was reassuring, always there, always moving. I find the river calming, relaxing, and it makes negotiating the Opryland Hotel area traffic worth the trouble.

I made some hot tea, strong, sweet and with a lot of lemon, put on an old light-blue fleece Titans pullover and took a blanket outside to the patio. I felt as if I needed fresh air, so I sat there as the air cooled quickly without the sun. The last heat rose from the patio stones.

From spring through fall the river was busy with boaters, waterskiers, riverboat dinner cruises, and water taxis. But now the river was quiet. Except for the occasional small plane from Cornelia Fort Airport across the river, I could have been a hundred miles from a city.

Cornelia Fort was a pioneer in women's aviation. Like Bitsy, she was the independent-minded socialite daughter of another prominent Nashville family. Cornelia had left her family's farm on the east side of the Cumberland to fly. She was a flight instructor in Honolulu when Pearl Harbor was bombed, actually in the air looking down on Japanese planes when the island was attacked.

Shortly after the attack on Pearl Harbor, she became one of the first pilots with the Women's Air Corps, ferrying planes to be flown in combat by men, and had died when another aircraft had crashed into hers. Women pilots were not considered fit for combat, but the story was, it had been a man who had accidentally flown his plane into Cornelia's.

Part of the farm that once was Cornelia's home is now a general aviation airport named for her. What would her life have been if she'd come home after the war? Would she have married, had children, taken up golf at the Club (which, by the way, was functioning back then and still doesn't allow women to be full members), settled back into Nashville life as Bitsy had seemed to? Would Cornelia have chaired balls? Would she still be making waves, pushing the boundaries as she had in aviation? What was lost to Nashville, to women, to everything Cornelia might have cared passionately about when her plane exploded over Texas?

I sat huddled under my blanket and sipped my tea and thought about Bitsy and the people who were missing her as long as I could take it while the pink faded from the sky.

FOUR

I wanna fly

Like an eagle takes to wing
I wanna fly
Can you hear me sing?
I wanna fly

Stick Anderson

t was after eight when Sam came by, but he didn't come empty-handed. When I opened the door, he stood there holding a pizza and a six pack of Cokes.

'Pepperoni, onions, mushrooms, and, just for you, anchovies.'

'You can't fool me, Detective. You got anchovies because you secretly like anchovies. But come in. That pizza's just getting cold out there.'

I had the gas log fire burning, and I had made an apple pie, so the house was warm and smelled like, well, apple pie. I wasn't trying to impress him, not really. I hadn't known he would come by, but I wasn't surprised.

I took the Cokes, and Sam followed me into the kitchen. He got plates while I put ice in glasses. Whenever Sam is here, he does whatever needs to be done. He doesn't sit down and wait to be served. Does that come from not having a wife? He doesn't live alone, though; he's a single father with a teenaged daughter living with him.

'How's Julie?'

'Great. All As last six weeks. She's decided she wants to go to Vanderbilt, and she can't do that without a scholarship. So these days she's studying.'

'Sounds good. Lofty goals, high aspirations.'

'Yeah, well, next week it will be UT or Harvard or Oregon.'

'Oregon?'

'She thinks it would be cool to say she's a Duck. She likes the idea of the Scottsdale Community College Fighting Artichokes, too.'

'Tell her she has to be careful about yellows and greens with her coloring.'

'That's a point. I'll tell her. That's the kind of rationale I think she'd find meaningful right now.'

Sam's daughter Julie is a lovely blonde, tall like her father, intelligent and a cheerleader at McGavock High School. I had found that she was a friend of my best friend MaryNell's daughter Melissa, who plays basketball for McGavock. I was now kept well informed on Detective Davis' activities. I knew, for instance, that, aside from occasionally seeing me, he didn't date anyone and that Julie consistently encourages him to 'get a life'.

Melissa said Julie liked me. I thought she probably felt I was her best chance to get him a little distracted from being such an involved parent and paying too close attention to her activities and friends. Julie is a good kid, but she is a teenager. Sam, however, to Julie's frustration, has continued to stay focused on his parenting, showing up at ball games, keeping in touch with teachers and, according to Julie by way of Melissa, scaring off boyfriends with 'that cop look'.

I knew what she meant. I had seen the cop look, and it scared me. Tonight, though, he just looked tired, his usually clear blue eyes cloudy with fatigue. I poured a Coke over ice and handed it to him. Maybe the caffeine would help.

'Thanks.'

'Do we eat first or detect first?'

'Eat. Pizza has a short half-life.'

We took the plates, napkins, pizza and Coke, paraphernalia of the modern instant supper, to my kitchen table. I set out some carrot sticks and dip. Every meal needs some vegetables. My table is set in a little bay off the kitchen, with a wall of windows curving around it. The walls, appliances and cabinets are white, but the oak floors and wood table and chairs keep it warm. It's a used kitchen. That night we were eating take-out pizza, but I do like to cook. Pots and utensils hang from a rack, and the copper pots are used too often to stay polished.

Even though it was night and still technically winter and we couldn't see the river any more, we could hear faint water sounds.

As we ate, Sam filled me in. Bitsy's car had been found at the airport in a long-term parking lot. The Spider was relatively clean. A couple of the children's art works were in the back, paper clips, pens, old receipts from Burger King and Whit's Barbecue. The normal detritus of the modern American driver. No stray French fries. She usually drove the Range Rover when she took the kids. The Spider was just for fun, just for her. There seemed to be fingerprints, but, in the normal driving position (ten and two, I can still hear my driver education teacher saying), there were no clear prints.

'My guess is,' Sam said, 'that whoever drove it last wore gloves. That would have smeared whatever prints were there. It's February, and the weather's been cold; nothing unusual about wearing gloves this time of year.

'There were a couple of pieces of pottery behind the seat, though,' he continued. 'Unfinished. Bisque, the husband said, fired once but not glazed yet.' Sam shrugged. 'He said she did pottery a lot, that it wouldn't be unusual to find the stuff around anywhere.'

I nodded. 'Yeah, she had her own studio behind the house. Sometimes she bought the pieces already poured and fired. There's a little place up in Joelton where she got it. She would paint and glaze the pieces, then refire them in her own kiln. Sometimes she did the whole piece herself from clay, usually something more artistic than functional. There's a gallery in Green Hills that sells some of her original pieces. I have a vase here that she gave me.'

I got up and went to the bedroom to get the vase from my desk. I brought it back, and held it out to Sam. 'I think it's incredible, although it needs flowers to look its best.'

The vase was irregularly shaped and looked like a patch of grass, the green all shades with browns and grays mixed in as in real life. There were hints of bugs in the grass, too, and a couple of dead leaves. With flowers, especially wildflowers or early spring blooms, the vase looked like a bit of the outdoors sitting on my desk, organic, too earthy to be cute. Bitsy had made it for me one spring, and I loved it.

Sam held the vase uncomfortably, turning it in his big hands. 'Nice. Now put it up before I break it.' I took the vase from him and put it on the table.

'Did she do this just for fun, a hobby, or did she sell her work?'

'A little of both. Like I said, there's a gallery that represents her, but she doesn't need the money, of course. She does it because she loves it, loves to get her hands in the clay.'

A parking receipt, which must have been plucked from an automated dispenser before the gate to the lot will open, had been found lying on the floor of Bitsy's Spider. It indicated that the car was parked on the day Bitsy was supposed to have left, about two hours before her flight's scheduled departure time. Seemed right. If the receipt had been for the day after the flight, that would have been suspicious. This looked like a traveler parked her car before she checked in for her flight. Normal. The car had been impounded, and the lab guys were checking the receipt for prints and going over the car with a fine-toothed vacuum. There was an original owner's manual in the glove compartment, decades old, a hairbrush, several road maps (actual paper maps, probably nearly as old as the owner's manual, left in the glove box after some old road trips), a garage door opener and a small packet of tissues between the seats. Nothing unusual.

We each cleared up our own debris. I put the dishes in the dishwasher and the leftover pizza and a couple of pieces of pie in plastic food bags for Sam to take home for himself and Julie. I'm not a fan of leftover pizza for breakfast; one of the things I have learned about Sam is that he is. We took coffee into the den, and I told my Alexa speaker to play Mickey Newbury.

Sam relaxed in my leather Scandinavian zero gravity recliner, which doesn't look it but is the most comfortable chair I have ever sat in. I saved months for that chair. Sam's legs were too long for the position of the ottoman, so he moved it farther from the chair. His arms and legs seemed to spill over the edges. His jacket was off, and the badge clipped to his belt caught the light.

'So, Campbell, tell me about this woman,' Sam said. 'Just talk about her for a while.'

I smiled and shook my head. How do you sum up a person on demand? I leaned my head back against the sofa pillows and closed my eyes. I started by describing Bitsy. I knew I was telling Sam a lot of things he already knew, and I knew he was sifting, waiting for the occasional nugget that he hadn't heard before.

'Well, her name doesn't fit.' Bitsy was tall. At some early adolescent point, she had outgrown her nickname. She was long-limbed and athletic, with fair skin and blonde hair. She played tennis and ran. In high school, I'd heard her say, and in college at a north-eastern Seven Sisters school, she had played lacrosse, a game I had never even seen played except on obscure cable channels when nothing else was in season. Even now, winter and summer, the bridge of her nose was sunburned because she was always doing something outdoors.

She was funny, intelligent, confident, but didn't take herself too seriously. 'Once I was at her house, and she put some paper take-out container in the oven to warm. I was shocked, asked her if she really wanted to catch the place on fire or something.' I looked at Sam. 'She said, "Don't you remember *Fahrenheit 451*? Paper burns at four hundred fifty-one degrees Fahrenheit. I set the oven at three seventy-five. Never underestimate the value of an over-priced liberal arts education," she said. She went on to tell me how she cleaned her silver. Instead of using silver polish, she put the tarnished silver in a sink lined with aluminum foil and filled with really hot water and non-iodized salt.' Sam's eyebrows rose, his face a question mark. 'The salt acts as a catalyst in a chemical reaction. You get pure silver plating back onto the piece and tarnished aluminum foil.' Sam laughed. 'I tried it. It works,' I insisted. 'She said it was the only thing of practical value she'd learned in chemistry class.'

I told Sam how our casual friendship had developed gradually over the years after our first meeting over Charlie's bad coffee. The first time I had done business for Bitsy was when I had planned a vacation for her and her husband Philip to San Francisco. I had recommended a small hotel on the bay that she had never heard of, not one of the larger, well-known, luxury hotels. I knew they'd have a view of the water from their king-sized bed. I had told her my favorite restaurants there, like Ernie's, and we discussed San Francisco shopping. I knew what to shop for and where to find it even if I couldn't afford to buy.

They'd had a great time. Bitsy had called to tell me how much they had loved the hotel. The five days and nights in San Francisco were the best time they'd spent together since their honeymoon, and she gave me part of the credit.

Bitsy had never complained about her marriage, but she was transparently excited and hopeful immediately after that trip. Weeks later, when she found that she had become pregnant in the little hotel on the bay, she sent me flowers.

'Bitsy and Philip met in college,' I explained to Sam. 'She was at Wellesley; Philip was at MIT,' which had, as MIT students were proud to say, the only business school in Boston, Harvard's being across the Charles River in Cambridge. 'Her roommate dated his roommate, and Bitsy and Philip naturally met. The roommates broke up, but Bitsy and Philip stuck. He was from near Evansville, Indiana. His father was a factory worker, I think. Definitely not Belle Meade.'

'How could he afford MIT?' Sam asked.

'Scholarships, loans.'

Sam was taking notes now. He put up his hand. 'Slow down. Gimme a chance to catch up.' I waited. 'OK, go on.'

'Bitsy said Philip was always in demand as a date for sorority socials because he looked so great in a tuxedo,' I continued. 'It made for great photographs. He looked great, period.'

Sam's expression was cynical.

Philip would have heard about Bitsy's deb ball and the parties surrounding it, but all that had happened before they met. He came home with her the year her mother chaired the Swan Ball, the event of Nashville's social year. Bitsy's gracious family must have been dazzling for the ambitious, small-town boy trying to get the blue out of his collar. White-tie and held annually at Cheekwood to benefit the Cheekwood Botanical Garden and Art Gallery, the Swan Ball attracted the highest of Nashville high society, only the hottest country music stars, and more than a few national figures.

'They got married after graduation and settled in Nashville. Philip was personable and good-looking in a blond, all-American way. He still doesn't sound Southern, but at least he didn't sound Yankee for long.' Philip had earned an MBA at Vanderbilt's Owen School of Business and went to work with a good brokerage firm. Bitsy joined the Junior League just as her mother had.

'Once,' I said, 'Bitsy said maybe it would have been better for them if they hadn't come back to Nashville, if they had gone anywhere but Nashville. If Philip had built a career of his own somewhere where he wasn't Everett Thompson's son-in-law, Bitsy Thompson's husband, where he could have been successful as himself.' I shrugged.

In time, Philip's name was put up for membership in the Club. In Nashville, no one needed to ask or explain which club. The Club was Belle Meade Country Club, and it took more than money to get in. Before too long, a prominent banker from an old Nashville family died peacefully of old age. 'Do you remember?' I asked Sam. 'The pictures and tributes were on the front page. The discreet announcement of Philip's invitation to join the Club was in the last paragraph of the next week's society column, when we still had a society column.'

Sam laughed.

Bitsy and Phil were regulars in the society pages, and Bitsy volunteered for all the most worthy causes. One year she chaired the Symphony Guild Ball; another year the Heart Gala. She was always on one Swan Ball committee or another, and she persuaded her garden club to sponsor a Habitat house. Its landscaping was the best on the street. Bitsy went back as the seasons changed to help the new homeowner, a single mother of three named Yolanda who worked in a shoe factory, make her garden a place of joy all year. Bitsy and Yolanda became friends, and Yolanda and her children were occasionally seen in Belle Meade.

'So I should talk to this Yolanda, too,' Sam said. 'Do you know her last name or an address?'

'No, I don't. I'm sure it would be in Bitsy's day planner.'
Sam made another note. 'And I'm sure Philip or her parents
could tell you. The house is off Brick Church Pike on a street
with several Habitat houses. I've been out there a few times.
I might be able to find it. They weren't best friends; I don't
mean to say that. But Bitsy had a way of collecting people
she met, and I mean that in the best possible way. If she liked
you, she didn't just let you go when your usefulness was over.
Once she had a birthday luncheon, and it was the oddest
assortment of women, all incomes, all ways of life, black,
white, all ages, but all interesting, and all people Bitsy
considered friends.'

'OK. What about the husband? What else do you know
about him?'

'Not much. Thompson, the son, was born two years after
Rachel, but no flowers then. Although Bitsy usually did bring
me a gift from any place she went that was unusual. Nothing
big or expensive, just a little something special so you'd know
she'd thought of you.

'She doesn't talk about Philip much in recent years. You
know how some women are always telling you something
their husbands have said, just in conversation, like Bill thinks
this or that; Bill hates Chinese food, whatever. Bitsy just
doesn't mention Philip often.'

'Do you ever see him, talk to him?'

'Once in a while. We do his business travel, too, but his
secretary usually arranges it. When he does come in, he has
to talk to everyone, even if we're busy. You want to tell him
it's OK, he doesn't have to be everybody's best friend. He's
always polite, really nice, but sometimes, I don't know, it's a
little too much. That's not fair,' I corrected myself. 'He's really
nice.'

'Does he travel much?'

'Not a lot. Once a month or so maybe, not much more than
that.'

'Would you get me copies of those records? Where he's
gone, when? Did he travel with anybody?'

I started to agree, then stopped.

'I'll be glad to get it together for you, but I think you'd

better get another subpoena to cover it. I don't want to be
sued because I gave out confidential information. And there
is some confidential information in those records, credit card
numbers, stuff like that.'

Sam nodded. 'OK. I'll come by tomorrow – or – I don't
know. How long will it take you to get it all together?'

'Probably not too long. I'll run an accounting report to get
the dates. Give me until afternoon.'

'What about the parents?'

'I don't really know them. I've met them a few times. Nice,
especially the mother. Very traditional. Her mother has that
distinctive West Nashville accent. You know what I mean?'
You don't hear it in the younger generation, but in women of
my mother's age and older who lived in Belle Meade and that
area of West Nashville, there's an accent that's different from
the rest of the city. Broader vowels. Softer r's. Older money.'

'Yeah, I know. I'd never thought about it before. Were
they . . .' Sam caught himself. 'Are they close?'

'Yes, very. Bitsy talks to her mother every day and sees her
nearly that often. When Mrs Thompson says Bitsy wouldn't
have left for two weeks and not told her or talked to her since
she's been gone, I'd say you can believe her.'

I realized I was using present tense. I hoped that wasn't just
wishful thinking.

'What about the father?'

'I haven't been around him much. Old money, on the board
at Belle Meade, the Sports Council, Children's Hospital, very
big in banking, very distinguished. I don't have any real reason
for this, but I always thought he was kind of controlling.'

I couldn't think of much else, and Sam left soon, taking his
care package of leftovers, after asking me to keep a notebook
with me for a while to write down anything I thought of about
Bitsy.

I followed him outside as he left, shivering in the February
night as I broke some evergreen stems, white pine and holly,
about all that was alive in my yard, to put in Bitsy's vase.

FIVE

Deep in winter's cold
It's the robin I miss

Stick Anderson

As soon as Sam left, I called a friend of mine who's a researcher for the *Tennessean*, now Nashville's only daily newspaper since the afternoon *Nashville Banner* shut down a few years ago. And it's part of a chain now, no longer the independent voice it was in the old days when John Seigenthaler was the legendary editor. Mark Allen is one of the few real investigative journalists left there, and sometimes I think his days are numbered. He generally knows everything that's going on in this town – or he knows how to find out. He's a holdover from the days when the *Tennessean* did serious, competitive investigative journalism. He's gone undercover to investigate a corrupt governor, investigated the KKK and laughed off death threats – or pretended to laugh them off. When people say he knows where the bodies are buried, he looks nervous. I suspect there's some literal truth to that. I asked what he had heard about Bitsy Carter.

'There'll be a story in tomorrow's paper – front page. Old Nashville family, husband's an outsider – even if he has lived and worked here for a dozen or so years. Young, pretty mother disappears, no trace. It's a story people will still buy newspapers for. The husband is the obvious suspect . . .'

'You're assuming somebody's done something to her, that she hasn't just disappeared.'

'I'm assuming she's been murdered. But you're right. That's not the only possibility. She could have run away, started a new life.'

'No, she couldn't. That doesn't leave any good possibilities, does it?'

'Not unless you're a fan of the amnesia plot so often used when a soap opera star needs time off to go to rehab, then comes back to the show. I haven't seen that happen much in real life. What do you have to do with this?'

I explained.

'Want to make a statement? There's still time to add it to tomorrow's edition.'

'No, thanks.'

'You're going to have reporters asking. You might as well be prepared. Just give it to me first; that's all I ask.'

'I don't want to talk about this to reporters, Mark.'

'You don't have to talk, but they'll be asking. It's their job. Look, I'll call you tomorrow. I'll tell you what's being said around here. You tell me what you've found out.'

'We'll see.'

SIX

The next morning I went by AAAAuto on Nolensville Road before I went to work. I wanted to check on the Spider. I had been taking it to Charlie at AAAAuto for service for years and not because AAAAuto was the first auto repair listing in the yellow pages. Charlie loved the Spider, too, and he had grieved with me when it was towed in, its once shiny red hood crumpled from its late-night impact with a tree on an icy hillside. Its trunk had been crunched by the Mercedes whose driver was trying to force me off the road. The Spider was slowly being rehabilitated, some parts being replaced, others patiently hammered back into shape with a rubber mallet.

Beyond the grease and car parts, behind the walls lined with fan belts and mismatched tires, are Charlie's clean rooms, the office where he keeps his computer and, beyond that, the paint room. He had spent hours poking around in the salvage yards on the side roads of the information superhighway, looking for the parts he couldn't fix.

'It's comin' along, Miz Hale. I been on the Internet. I found two carburetors from the same model in Wenatchee, Washington, yesterday. They'll be here in a week. That was a piece of luck. It's tough to find those carburetors; they're twin-choke and fit in horizontal, so you can't just take something from another car and make it work.'

'That's great, Charlie. What's left?'

He ran his hand gently over the crumpled fender. 'Well, you can see there's a lot of body work. I think I can rebuild the camshaft, but I'm still looking for a crank case.'

'I appreciate your doing it, Charlie. I miss it.'

'I know you do, Miz Hale. I'll be glad to see the day you can drive it home.'

'Thanks, Charlie. Oh, Charlie, have you done any work on Mrs Carter's Spider lately?'

'Not much. I seen her, oh, maybe last month for an oil change.'

'OK, thanks. What do I owe you so far?'

He waved off my thanks and my question. 'We'll talk about it. I'll let you know when I need some money.'

That's how Charlie does business. He's an anachronism, I suppose, doing business on trust and a handshake. I was glad I had found him.

'Said she was bringing it back for me to take a look at the engine,' Charlie had dismissed money and was back to Bitsy, 'but she never did. Then I saw in the paper how she was missin'.' He shook his head. 'It's a mean world.'

I nodded. What was there to say? 'She left the Spider at the airport, you know. It was in the long-term lot.'

'She never!' Charlie had been sad before; now he was in shock, outraged at the very idea. 'She never would of left that car in an airport parking lot and gone outta the country. Somethin' happened to that girl before that car wound up there. She wouldn't'a done that. No, sir!'

I left AAAAuto wondering if I should tell Sam what Charlie thought.

SEVEN

At work, I warned everyone not to give out any information on the Carters except to the police. 'Just say that it would be unethical of us to discuss anyone who might or might not be a client. That's it. Nothing more.'

I ran a report from the accounting program showing all the activity in Phil Carter's account and in Phil and Bitsy's personal account going back to the beginning of last year. There were fifteen transactions in Phil's business account. Armed with the dates and invoice numbers, I went to the files and pulled the invoices.

Most of Phil Carter's travel was unremarkable. He had made six trips to New York, three to Los Angeles, two to Chicago, two to Indianapolis. Twice, though, once last April and again in November, Philip Carter had gone to Zihuatanejo. Alone. Or, at least, no one else had been ticketed on the invoices with him. There was no hotel reservation on either invoice. I went back to the files and looked through all the invoices for tickets issued the same days as Carter's plus those from a few days before and after. Nothing else for Zihuatanejo. Lee had run one ticket; Anna had issued the other.

I made copies for Sam and another set for myself. I talked to Lee and Anna, but they couldn't remember anything unusual about the transactions. I went back to Martha.

'When Bitsy Carter called, did she talk about Zihuatanejo, about why she wanted to go there?'

'As far as I remember, we didn't talk much. She just said she wanted to go to a spa she'd heard of in that area; she couldn't remember the name or exactly where it was.'

'Did she mention Philip, her husband?'

'Maybe. I'm not sure. Somebody had told her about the spa. She didn't say a whole lot. I remember thinking that she was always so friendly and talkative when she came in here to see you, but that day she wasn't. I just remember thinking she must have been in a hurry or really busy.'

I couldn't see any pattern or anything unusual except those two trips to the west coast of Mexico, and I had no idea what they meant. I would exchange the records for Detective Davis' subpoena and let him earn my tax money.

EIGHT

Deep in winter's cold

It's the robin I miss
Bluebirds and wrens
Building nests for their babies
Homes for hungry chicks
But when I melt in the sun
I watch for the birds flying high
Surfing the sky
Because when I see them

I wanna fly
Like an eagle takes to wing
I wanna fly
Can you hear me sing?
I wanna fly

Stick Anderson

The next day Sam called. 'Can you meet me for lunch?'
'Sure,' I said.
'Meet me at the Lipscomb baseball field at noon. The university, not the high school.'

That wasn't quite what I had expected, but it was another great day, warm and sunny. People kept saying it was hard to believe it was February, and I was finding it hard to believe that it was baseball season already. It occurred to me that in college the boys of summer must play a lot of games in cold, wind, even sleet and snow. That day, though, was a day that was made for being outside, warming my winter-pale face in the sun, watching baseball played outside on real grass for the love of the game. And the Lipscomb campus was pretty convenient to my office, tucked in a Green Hills residential area with a street curving around the outfield. Occasionally, long fly balls were a driving hazard.

When I got to the field, Sam had left a ticket for me at the gate. He was at the concession stand ordering lunch.

'Hi. Relish?'

'Yes, everything.'

'Coke?'

'Yes, thanks. I'll carry the drinks.'

We found seats between home and first. There were about fifty others there in fleece hoodies, sweatshirts and coats, some parents, several students, some obviously businessmen who would be heading back to nearby offices soon. The game was starting early because it was a double-header, and I assumed there would be more students in the stands later as they finished classes for the day.

The home team, in white that contrasted sharply against the bright, new-green grass, was warming up on the field. Their purple-and-gold hats stood out like early crocus. The outfield was lined with hedge and fit into the curve of the residential street that bordered it. A coach was hitting practice balls to outfielders, the crack of his bat a sharp counterpoint to the softer *whump* of balls in gloves. White balls drew arcs over the green grass. The school's colors are purple and gold, and this team sported those colors proudly. There was one legendary coach, though, years ago when the school's teams played in the NAIA instead of the NCAA, who thought all baseball should be played in pinstripes. They consistently made it to the NAIA World Series, so nobody wanted to get rid of him. They let him have his way, and Lipscomb players wore their navy-and-white pinstripes under their purple-and-gold jackets in championship games.

I breathed deeply. The air was clean and fresh with the spring smell of new-mown grass. 'You come here often?'

Sam looked at me sideways and grinned. 'Yeah, I do, as a matter of fact. I like baseball. This is a good program. Back in the seventies, before the Sounds and Titans and Preds came, it was the best game in town.' Sam referred to Nashville's triple-A professional baseball team and professional football and hockey teams. 'You can usually count on a good game, especially when they're playing Belmont, like today. It's a great place to spend an hour on a nice day, and the hot dogs aren't bad. Battle of the Boulevard.'

Lipscomb and Belmont are small, private liberal arts universities a mile or so apart on the same street in Nashville, Belmont Boulevard. Supported by different churches, the schools have been rivals for decades. Belmont students were often accused of sneaking on campus to paint the statue of the Bison, the Lipscomb mascot, in the old days on the night before a big game. Lipscomb students have been known to return the minor vandalism. Now Lipscomb students repaint the big Bison regularly.

Once, though, in a misguided fervor of partisan biblical correctness, the statue of John the Baptist on the Belmont campus had been beheaded. There were apologies and diplomatic clean-up teams. Things had cooled after that.

'How's your investigation going?' I asked.

Sam frowned. 'Philip Carter says he first went to Zihuatanejo to check out some manufacturing company in the area for investment potential. He told his wife about it, about the spa there, Quetzalcoatl?' Sam stumbled over the pronunciation. 'He went back a second time but decided the Mexican business was too unstable for him to recommend. So, no record of any investments or recommendations to corroborate his story. He says his wife decided to go there because he told her about the spa. Thought she'd like it. So, no unusual coincidence. Nothing there to prove or disprove.'

'It sounds plausible enough,' I said. 'The thing is, Martha said Bitsy was vague about the spa. Looks like she would have just asked Philip for the name.'

'Yeah. The whole thing is not right somehow. I just can't figure out how.'

From the press box above and behind us, the announcer was calling out the Lipscomb starting lineup as the players ran to their positions on the field. The pitcher threw a few last warm-up pitches as the Belmont lead-off batter approached the plate.

'What do the parents say?' I asked.

'The mother thinks "something happened" to her. They're sending a private detective to Mexico.'

The first batter popped out. The second was swinging at anything, looking determined to hit one over the hedge that lined the street.

'Think they'll find anything?'

The second batter was out, frustration mixed with the dust on his face as he stalked back to the dugout.

'I don't know. Probably not. People can just disappear there, whether they want to or not. We have this idea that being a United States citizen keeps us safe somehow, that the government protects us wherever we go, but that's just not true. A rich woman tourist alone in Mexico, most people are going to think she was asking for something to happen. Whatever is wrong with the US legal system, it's a lot better than most of the world.'

Just then the third batter hit a long drive to a hole in left center. It looked like a sure double, maybe a triple, but the Lipscomb left fielder dove and, flying horizontal in the air, caught it just before he and the ball hit the ground. He bounced and rolled, but he came up with the ball, holding his glove high as he ran in toward the dugout. Three up, three down.

'So what do you do next?' I asked.

'We have an open missing person investigation. I probably wouldn't be involved in it, not yet anyway, with no more to go on than we have so far, except the banker father owns half the politicians in town and a few in Washington.' Sam was a homicide detective, so he wasn't ordinarily involved in missing person investigations until there was a reasonable probability that the missing person was dead. 'I do what I do, ask questions, follow up to see if the answers are true. The thing is, this smells bad. Lots of people have bad marriages, probably lots of the couples you see walking around wouldn't be grief-stricken if one or the other disappeared. But they don't murder each other. So it's not that any husband who isn't crazy with concern must be a murderer. There are just too many questions here, and when I have a lot more questions than answers, I get suspicious.'

The left fielder who had just made the spectacular catch, number eleven, was swinging a bat in the on-deck circle below us. He tapped the bat against the inside of each cleat as he waited. The batter swung, hit the ball low and popped it up. Automatic out. Infield fly.

'You see, I hate that! You should have to play it out.'

Sam turned to me. 'What?'

'The infield fly rule. If you hit a fly in the infield with runners on first and second on the third Tuesday after a full moon with a rabbit's foot in your left shoe . . . It's a wimpy rule.'

Sam looked at me with a bemused look on his face. 'I had no idea you cared so strongly about baseball.'

'I just think if you're gonna play the game, you ought to play the game. The infield fly rule is like little kids playing in the backyard, and the kid who owns the ball gets to make up the rules.'

The left fielder came up, dug in first his left foot then the right beside the plate. He let the first pitch, a strike, go by him. The second one, though, he hit over the fence. Sam tried patiently to explain the reasons for the infield fly rule: the infielder could intentionally miss or drop the ball and be almost assured a double play.

'So don't hit flies in the infield,' I retorted with the self-righteous assurance of someone who had never faced a pitcher of higher caliber than one of those backyard kids, who had never seen a ball coming at her face at ninety miles an hour.

He grinned and shook his head. Sam, it turned out, had played high school and college baseball. He said he had played first and had been an 'all right' hitter. I could imagine those long arms stretching up and out to bring in any ball that came near first base.

We ate our hot dogs in the winter sun. Lipscomb was up by three when it was time for me to go back to work.

NINE

E ven though I was busy, the day dragged. All afternoon, my mind kept going back to Bitsy alone in Mexico. I was working with three college medical mission groups planning to go to Central America for their spring break. Not your typical wild college kids out to drink a swath through a beach town. They would have a long layover in Houston, so I arranged for a meeting room at the airport where they could crash – maybe not the best choice of words in that context – between flights. I called the group leaders to reconfirm that the names they had given me were official passport names. I planned to issue the tickets in about a week, and I wanted to give them time to check.

Late in the afternoon, things had slowed down. I was caught up, and for once the phones weren't ringing.

Idly, I picked up the worldwide *Hotel & Travel Index*, not as easy as it sounds since it probably weighs fifteen to twenty pounds, and found the spa resort outside Zihuatanejo where Bitsy had gone. Besides the listing with the current manager's name, the address, phone and fax numbers, website and email address, a range of rates which never seemed to correspond to actual rates you're quoted, there was a quarter page ad.

> Spa Quetzalcoatl. A place for renewal.
> A Full Service Spa for Fitness and Rejuvenation. Special and Custom Diet Plans available on request. Mud and Herbal Treatments. Mineral Water Baths. Swedish, Reflexology and Acupressure Massage. Come Alive Again.

The photo showed a beautiful woman lying in the sun being offered a drink by a dark-skinned, good-looking, white-uniformed attendant. A pool glistened nearby with purple mountains in the background.

Yes, I could come alive there, I thought. But what about Bitsy?

Then I went to a different book, just as big and almost as heavy. This one didn't include any paid advertising, and hotels couldn't pay to be listed in it. Theoretically, it included unbiased reviews of hotels and resorts, and I had found its information pretty reliable.

The Spa Quetzalcoatl was a five-star property, known as much for its discretion as for the obvious luxury. Expensive and popular with Southern Californians and celebrities who wanted privacy for their weight loss or drying out or recovery from cosmetic surgery, the spa offered a full range of diet, exercise and relaxation facilities. Medical staff were on site twenty-four hours a day. Regimented programs were offered, but you could also go there and do nothing. Privacy was ensured.

That's how Bitsy could have been registered there for two weeks without either being seen or arousing interest. That was the specialty of Spa Quetzalcoatl.

On Mexico's west coast it would be mid-afternoon now.

TEN

I decided to call the spa. Zero 11 for international calling, then Mexico's 52 code, then 755 and the number. Too many chances to go wrong with a number that long. There was a toll-free 800 number, but that was probably just a reservation service in the States. I wanted to talk to someone on site at the hotel, someone who was there. There was a long, buzzing ring.

'*Hola*. Spa Quetzalcoatl.'

'*Hola*. May I speak to the *administrator*, *por favor*?'

'*Sí. Uno momento*.'

I held.

'*Sí*, hello. This is Maria Sanchez.'

'Maria. This is Campbell Hale.' I gave the name of the agency and told her that I was in Nashville.

'*Sí*. Yes. How may I help you?' Her English was accented, but excellent.

'Bitsy Carter, actually Mary Elizabeth Carter, is a client of ours.'

'Ah, *sí*, *la desparecida*. Her parents have called here and her husband. I am sorry, Mrs Hale, but we have no idea where *Señora* Carter is.'

'I know you've been asked about this before, and I'm sorry to bother you, but she is a client and a friend, and this is so unlike her. Do you mind talking to me about it?'

'I am sure you know of our reputation for discretion. We are quite protective of it; it is much of what our clients pay for. However, in this case, there is really nothing for me to tell you, I'm afraid.'

'I understand. Her family is extremely worried about her.' I explained about Thompson's birthday.

'*Sí*, yes, of course, I am glad to talk to you. I do not think, though, that I will be beneficial. I have questioned the agent who was on duty when Mrs Carter checked in, but she cannot remember her.'

'What is your normal check-in procedure?'

'Ordinarily, a guest or her agent calls or faxes her arrival time, and one of our drivers picks her up at the airport in Zihuatanejo. If a guest doesn't wish to be seen in the lobby, the driver comes inside to fetch her key and takes her directly to her *casa*.'

'What about payment?'

'That would already have been arranged in advance. In this case, as in most, the payment was by credit card. It was already arranged before Mrs Carter arrived.'

'What about meals?'

'Many guests dine in their *casas*, and there are two dining rooms, one of which offers only diet cuisine. Guests can request special diets, usually in advance, but we don't insist on that. Some of our guests who are dieting don't wish to see the steaks, the sauces, the rich and tempting desserts. If a guest is not following a scheduled regimen, her privacy is respected. No one asks where she is eating or when. And meals are pre-paid.'

'So it's possible that no one would have seen Mrs Carter or talked to her except the driver?'

'*Sí*, if that is what she wished.'

'Would it be possible for me to speak to the driver?'

'Yes, of course, but he is not here now. He has gone into Zihuatanejo to the airport. He should be back in, ah, an hour and a half.'

'Thanks. I may call back then.'

'Of course. His name is Manuel. I must tell you, though, that I have already talked to him. He said he could not remember much about Mrs Carter. He wasn't sure, but he thought she wore a scarf that covered her hair and, indeed, much of her face. That is not at all uncommon for our guests if they do not wish to be recognized or if they have bruising from surgery, so he may be confused. And I cannot say for sure that it is actually Mrs Carter he is remembering. We are quite busy at this time of the year, and it has been two weeks. I'm sorry.'

'Yes, I understand. Look, Maria, if you think of anything, anything odd, anything at all, would you get in touch with me?' I gave her my phone and fax numbers as well as my email address and thanked her.

Just before I left for the day, Mark called.

'If you'll feed me supper, I'll tell you what I'm hearing.'

'You're accepting bribes now? OK. What time?'

'I'll be through about six thirty. So, about seven?'

'Sure.'

ELEVEN

In the soft summer night

I touch the blue velvet sky
Close as you are to me
And warming me in the moon's light
I feel you beside me
Touching my skin
You're home, and you're safe
The one I come home to
But this is the time when

I wanna fly

I stopped on the way home and picked up ribeye steaks and salad stuff. I got a half pound of the gourmet salad mix with assorted baby greens, some bleu cheese and a *Tennessean*.

When I got home, I switched on the local news and listened with half an ear while I started supper. I rinsed and drained the baby salad greens, put them on salad plates, sprinkled the bleu cheese on top and put the salads in the refrigerator to chill.

I mixed olive oil, basil vinegar, salt, pepper, a little sugar and garlic in a bottle. I looked through my spices and found some thyme and basil I had grown and dried last summer and added them. I shook the mixture and put it in the refrigerator. I made iced tea and sliced lemons.

The anchors chatted with each other and changed expression and tone as they segued from a multiple fatality wreck on I-65 to an international adoption to allegations of improprieties in a major state contract being awarded to a friend of the governor.

I crushed a couple of garlic cloves and put them in a shallow bowl with some wine to marinate the steaks. Then I saw Bitsy's photograph projected behind the anchors.

'A local mother of two is missing, and her prominent family is baffled.' The male anchor was solemn. 'More after these messages.'

In reality, there was very little more factual information after the messages. The names, the dates, videotape of Bitsy's car, of Philip and the children, of the Thompsons, Bitsy's mother and Philip appealing for information from anyone who might have seen anything and, at the story's close, a photo of Bitsy, smiling and happy.

When Mark came, I asked him to put the steaks on the grill while I set the table and put everything else together. He filled me in on what the *Tennessean*'s police beat reporter had learned and the rumors that were floating around.

Philip Carter, with his very good job with Nashville's most reputable brokerage firm, made very little on commissions.

'He doesn't have many long-term clients,' Mark said, 'because he apparently isn't a very good broker.'

I stopped adding cherry tomatoes and cucumber slices to the salads and looked at him.

'Buys high, sells low.'

'That would do it,' I agreed.

'But he brings in lots of new clients. He's a likable guy, plays a lot of golf. I guess people figure he has all this money, he must be doing something right. He brings in clients; they pair him with somebody less personable, maybe a young guy who hasn't had time to build a client roster, but with a lot more knowledge of the market. Carter gets a finder's fee. Eventually the new account is handled entirely by someone else.'

'How did he get a job with a firm like that?' I asked. 'How does he keep it? What's more important – how can I get a job like that?'

Mark laughed. 'That firm handles his father-in-law's impressively large portfolio. Most of the partners are old friends of Bitsy's father, all members of the Club. I guess they figure it's not such a bad deal. He brings in new people. They don't have to waste the time of bright but less well-connected guys.

Philip plays in every pro-am and celebrity golf tournament in town and most of the charity ones, so the company's name is out there. They get some credit for supporting good causes and private schools in the area. He photographs well. He's apparently a nice guy. Everybody likes him.'

'Who's everybody?'

'You know, people he works with, people who've played golf with him, hunted with him. I called some people.'

In that way men have of knowing other men for years, working with each other every day, but never discussing an intimate issue, other brokers said Philip was a regular guy.

'He's always good for a spare ticket to a Vandy or Titans game or a seat in Bitsy's father's Predators box,' Mark said. 'Takes people hunting in deer season and duck season on some farm property the Thompsons have.'

'Where is it?' I asked.

'Somewhere down in Maury County, between Franklin and Columbia.' Mark shrugged. 'Since Philip didn't go to school around here, he doesn't have to take sides when Ensworth plays Montgomery Bell Academy or when Vandy plays Tennessee. He never makes anybody mad, just a regular guy. You ask people about his marriage, and they look blank. They say, "OK, I guess. Bitsy's beautiful", but that's not unusual. Men don't talk about their marriages. A man can be two months into divorce proceedings before he mentions it to a guy he's been sitting with in a duck blind all day.'

I nodded and set the salads on the table.

'He's not making money on commissions,' Mark continued, 'and he's not making money on his own in the market. He seems to have absolutely no sense of timing. There's no way he'd still have that job if it weren't for Mr Thompson.'

'So what does he live on?'

'He gets a base salary, the finder's fees, but that wouldn't support the Carters' lifestyle. The house was a gift from Bitsy's parents – to Bitsy. It's in her name. The cars, word is they were paid for by the Thompsons, too. The children's private school tuition, you guessed it, paid by the Thompsons. A lot of grandparents pay private school tuitions, though.'

'You know,' I mused, 'I remember Bitsy using a credit card that her father paid. Sometimes a tour company or cruise line requires just the number, sometimes a billing address. I have a couple of credit card numbers for Bitsy. The billing address for one is her own; the bill for the other goes to her parents. That's the one she always used for major trips.'

'What about this trip, the Zihuatanejo thing?' Mark asked.

'I don't know. I'll check. You can't print this, you know.'

'Campbell!'

'Well, you can't. I can't be telling the newspapers how clients pay.'

'You just did,' he argued.

'No, I didn't,' I retorted. 'I told my friend in confidence.'

'I hate it when you do that.'

I shrugged, and we ate. In silence.

'Good steak,' he offered finally, making peace.

I nodded. 'You know what bothers me about this?'

Mark raised an eyebrow as he chewed.

I went on. 'What you've told me makes him sound like a dummy, like some good-looking, not too smart dolt. This man went to MIT on a scholarship, which means he had to have kept good grades, had to have been pretty smart, and he got an MBA from Owens. You can't do that without having something on the ball.'

Mark shrugged. 'What do you think happened?'

'It's possible that she went to Zihuatanejo,' I said, 'checked in at the spa, wandered off somewhere on her own, and was attacked. That happens in Mexico. That even happens in Nashville occasionally.'

'Yeah, but we usually find a body. And there's usually some very apparent reason: drugs, robbery, rape.'

'Usually, not always. And, if something happened to Bitsy in Mexico, it could have been for those same reasons. We just don't know. Charlie, the guy who works on her car, same guy who works on mine, you know?' Mark nodded. 'He doesn't think she'd have left her Spider at the airport. No matter how distraught she was. I don't know.' I pushed a radicchio leaf around my plate.

'And . . . I don't mean to sound crass here, Campbell. I

know she was a friend of yours. But, so far, nobody's found a body.'

'Yeah, and that's good news, right? I mean, maybe she's been in an accident somewhere and her jaw's wired shut, or she hasn't regained consciousness.'

'Or she has amnesia. I think I mentioned that. Amnesia always works for the soaps.'

'I'm serious, Mark. As long as there's no body, Schrodinger's Cat, she could be alive, maybe kidnapped.'

'Maybe, but don't count on it. The odds are, if she didn't disappear deliberately, she's probably dead. I'm sorry, but those are the two most likely possibilities. Are you really so sure she wouldn't have disappeared on her own? No lover?'

Suddenly the smell of the steak and the juices running red weren't so appealing. I realized I had lost my appetite and pushed the half-eaten, really good steak away. 'Well, yeah. I can believe she'd leave her husband. Who really knows what goes on in a marriage? Every year or two I hear of some marriage I thought was rock solid and blissfully happy breaking up, so I can believe anyone leaving a husband. But I can't believe Bitsy would leave her children.'

'Mexico would be an easy place to lose yourself. We're asking around to see if anybody's heard of her trying to get fake identification. We're also trying to find out if she withdrew cash before she left. We can't just ask the bank like your detective buddy.'

'In a way, I wish I could believe it, but I can't.'

TWELVE

I wanna fly

Like an eagle takes to wing
I wanna fly
Can you hear me sing?
I wanna fly

Stick Anderson

After Mark left, I decided to email the manager of the Spa Quetzalcoatl. She might not see the message until tomorrow, but, with the time difference, if she were working a little late, she might still be there. I looked up the spa in a hotel guide I keep at home.

From: Campbell Hale
To: Maria Sanchez
Subject: Mary Elizabeth T. Carter
Maria – Did Mrs Carter request a driver to take her anywhere after she checked in? Thanks.

Backspace.

Gracias for your assistance.

Half an hour later I had mail.

There is no record of Mrs Carter leaving or asking for a driver. In fact, there is no record of Mrs Carter making any request or contacting the desk after she checked in. There is also a shuttle that makes hourly trips into the village. Guests often take that rather than request a private

driver. There would be no record if Mrs Carter had taken
the shuttle. I will ask each driver tomorrow to be sure there
was no request that was not recorded by the front desk.

Fair enough.

THIRTEEN

T hat weekend was a slow, catching-up one. I noticed in
the Saturday morning paper that Lipscomb had won
both games of its double-header against Belmont the
day before. I did laundry and the jobs I always put off: hemmed
a new pair of slacks; changed the light bulbs outside that I
can't get to without a ladder; did my toe nails; exfoliated my
heels. My percussionist friend Stick Anderson was out of town
on tour with Chris Stapleton, so he wasn't available. I called
my friend MaryNell to see if she wanted to go to a movie,
but she had plans with her husband. 'Why not call the
detective?' she asked. I ignored her.

I vacuumed the refrigerator coils, all the while not letting
go of the idea of Bitsy arriving in Zihuatanejo with her face
covered and then disappearing. Bitsy not wanting to be seen
might not have seemed odd to the spa staff. They were used
to guests behaving that way. But Bitsy hadn't just had cosmetic
surgery; Bitsy wasn't a celebrity needing to protect her privacy.
Why would Bitsy have been hiding her face on the other side
of the continent? The weekend dragged.

FOURTEEN

O n Monday morning I drove to work in rain, listening to
the drive-time traffic reports of wrecks all over town: two
on I-24 inbound from Smyrna; one at I-65 and Concord

Road, south of town; another at I-65 and Trinity Lane to the north; one at I-40 at the Demonbreum exit; and, as usual, two on Briley Parkway near the Cumberland Bridge. Nashville in the rain.

At the office, there was a fax from Maria and the Spa Quetzalcoatl waiting for me. None of the drivers remembered any request by Mrs Carter to be driven back to the airport, to the city or anywhere else. One more dead end.

Bitsy had paid for her trip with the card which was billed to her father, though, as I thought more about it, I decided that told me nothing. The number was in her account profile. Martha would have asked which card to put it on, and Bitsy would have said 'the Visa' or 'the American Express.'

I spent the morning planning spring break trips and wishing I were getting out of town myself. I spent far too long with a woman who wanted a direct, non-stop flight to Billings, Montana. She couldn't understand why I insisted there wasn't one. She had flown to Billings before, and the plane was full. Why wouldn't the airlines just fly there?

I tried to explain the hub system. I tried to explain that if she flew American, she'd go through Chicago, and other people wanting to go to Billings from other cities would go to Chicago, so the airline would have enough passengers to fly to Billings. In the end, she decided I didn't know what I was talking about. She decided to call another agency. In the end, I was glad.

FIFTEEN

In the soft, summer night
I touch the blue velvet sky

Stick Anderson

S am called about eleven, just as I was beginning to think about lunch.

'You're not going to a ball game today, are you?' I

asked, watching the rivulets of rain pour down the windows at the front of the office.

'Nope. Rainout. Some are called on account of rain, you know.'

'That's what I've heard. Any news about Bitsy?'

'Not a lot. It seems she emptied a joint money market account.'

'How much was in it?'

'Not much. Just over twenty thousand.'

'Twenty thousand. Not much?'

'She had another account in her name only with almost a hundred thousand. She had some relatively liquid stocks that make that look like small change.'

I blinked. 'OK. Well, that looks like she intended to be back.'

'And the twenty thousand? Any thoughts on that?'

I thought. 'No. Could it have been a coincidence? An account she wanted to move, reinvest?'

'Maybe. But, if so, she didn't discuss it with her husband, whose name was also on the account, or her parents. And, besides, I don't believe in coincidences.'

'Never?'

'Almost never,' Sam reaffirmed.

'It could just be some reason like that was the easiest to access or the most convenient bank location, something like that, you know, that bank's on the way to the cleaners. Or it could be that she took that money because it was a joint account. Maybe she was mad at Philip. Either way, if she hadn't intended to be back, she would have taken everything, wouldn't she?'

'You'd think so.'

'Or it could be that's the only account Philip had access to, right?'

'Could be.'

After lunch, I answered the phone to hear Philip Carter's voice.

'Campbell? This is Phil Carter.'

'Hello.' I'm sure my surprise showed in my voice. 'I-I've heard about Bitsy, of course. Is there any news?'

'No, nothing.' His voice was heavy and tired, the voice of a man who hadn't gotten a lot of sleep lately.

'I'm so sorry. How are your children doing?'

'I don't know. I don't know how any of us are doing. They've spent a lot of time with friends; their friends' parents have been great. They can almost feel normal, maybe, without stumbling over police and investigators and photographers.' I was reaching for something comforting, but Philip continued. 'I know they have to do their jobs. I'm grateful for it. We want them to keep Bitsy's picture out there in front of people, but I can't help feeling it's too much for the kids. Our house is like a command station.'

'That has to be hard.'

'Yeah, well . . .' His voice trailed off. 'Anyway, the reason I'm calling is, I know the police have talked to you, I mean I'm sure they must have. I just thought, if there's anything you can do, anything you can think of that might help . . . I don't know. I just know that Bitsy liked and trusted you. I thought maybe she might have said something, maybe something that didn't mean anything at the time. Maybe even something about me, something about our marriage. Some reason she'd want to disappear.'

'I'm sorry, Philip. I didn't actually book this trip for her, and I hadn't talked to her in a few weeks. I was out the day she called in.'

'Oh.' He sounded – what? Disappointed? Surprised?

'I'm sorry. I have talked to the police, but I'm afraid we weren't much help.'

'Of course. Look, I'm sorry to bother you. I just thought maybe, I don't know, I guess I'm a little desperate.'

'Of course. I'm glad you called. I'd wanted to tell you and Bitsy's parents how concerned I am and that I've been thinking of you all, but I didn't want to intrude. If there's anything I can do, please call.'

'Thanks. I don't know. I've thought about going to Mexico myself, see if I can find out anything, but we're sending an investigator. I'm sure he can do better than I could. If I decide to go, I'll call you.'

'Of course. Call me anytime.' I gave him my cell number.

'I'm not sure the police would want me to go out of the country.' He laughed uneasily. 'I'm probably a suspect. The husband is always the first suspect.'

'I'm sure they have to look at everyone, everything,' I soothed.

'Yeah, yeah, and that's what I want, of course. Well, I'll let you go, Campbell, thanks for listening.'

Philip's call left me unsettled. He seemed to be in pain. He sounded as if he wanted everything done to find his wife. I really didn't want to think about how bad this was for him, for Bitsy's parents and for those children. Philip's call had made that very real. I should let Sam know about the call, I thought. I decided I'd call him later that afternoon.

By mid-afternoon, things had slowed a bit, and I pulled out the information on Spa Quetzalcoatl. Come alive again. The quetzalcoatl, where had I heard of that? Some sort of animal god, something to do with a bird? Why did I associate it with the phoenix, rising from its own ashes?

Idly, I logged onto the internet and put Ixtapa into the search engine. Ixtapa was a relatively new resort town developed near the older, smaller fishing village of Zihuatanejo. Hotels, history, local news, weather, shopping, attractions. What did I want to know?

The Spa Quetzalcoatl had its own site, very up-to-date. I went there first. The site was tasteful, restrained, the pages uncluttered. I took a virtual tour, peeking electronically into luxurious guest rooms and *casitas*, watching the woman from the ad rejuvenating by the pool as the young man actually served her a frosty drink. She adjusted her wide-brim hat, her body language suggesting total relaxation and indulgence. Again, the resort's discretion was emphasized.

I saw chefs preparing gourmet meals, each dish a carefully composed piece of art. I virtually stood in the lobby and in a guest room and virtually turned three hundred sixty degrees to look all around my virtual self. I was convinced. I wanted to be there instead of here in Nashville in the winter rain.

Next I went to attractions. Shopping? A list of village shops with owners and addresses, a streetscape. It looked like a pleasant place to wander for an afternoon. It looked real, a little too rundown to be quaint. Clothing, T-shirts, fishing and boating supplies, a few upscale tourist shops, silver. Snorkeling, sailing, wind surfing, scuba diving, golf, nightlife.

Sport fishing? Before the big hotels and resorts of Ixtapa, Zihuatanejo's reason for existing had been fishing. I found a site for a charter company, Zihuatanejo Fishing Charters. There were photographs of the fleet, six boats, shining white against the impossibly blue water. There was a photograph of the owners, a tanned and athletic Anglo couple smiling from the deck of the newest boat, the *Marlin's Blues*. Current weather and water conditions were listed. Cool mornings with afternoon highs just touching ninety degrees. Sunny. Oh, yes.

There were color photographs and descriptions of each boat, from the twenty-five-foot *Yellow Jack* to the thirty-six-foot *Marlin's Blues*. The boats were crewed, fully equipped with modern electronic navigational equipment, fighting chairs (that was an interesting idea), and bathrooms. They supplied ice and coolers, food and drinks. Coolers to ice the fish the fishermen brought home to cook or mount as well as coolers for the drinks. Not a cheap way to spend the day, but the rates didn't seem unreasonable when split between four or six fishermen. Zihuatanejo Fishing Charters encouraged sport fishermen to tag and release the fish they caught and even sponsored an annual tag and release tournament.

I clicked on the company blog. Last week had been a good week. The blog described fishing conditions – excellent, of course – what fish were being caught where, weather – perfect – how many yellowtail jacks, how many snapper, grouper, dorado and sailfish were taken by which boats.

Even more interesting, the blog told who caught which fish. No first names, just last. Mr Anderton from Red Island, Michigan, had caught a two-hundred-ninety-seven-pound black marlin about twenty miles offshore. Mr Henri from Lyon, France, fishing on the *Marlin's Blues* had taken a sailfish. The guests probably enjoyed the idea of others reading about them. They probably printed out the blogs for scrapbooks. I decided it was a good idea. And a great marketing tool.

Next, I clicked on the blog archives. Blogs from the past eight weeks were available, so I chose the one for the week that included the day of Bitsy's outbound flight. No mention of her, but I hadn't really expected that. In fact, that blog actually covered only a day or two of time that Bitsy might have been there. I exited that one and clicked on the next one.

It was dated ten days after Bitsy had disappeared and covered the week prior to that date. The weather had been warm: partly cloudy, cool mornings with afternoon highs from eighty-five to ninety, light winds. Sea conditions had been calm, and the bait supply of mackerel and bonito had been good. The best fishing area had been one to ten miles offshore with blue water in the bay.

And there, in the company of Mr Taylor of Tucson, Mr and Mrs Luke of Tupelo and Gulfport, Mr Sakasegawa and Mr Hirota of Tokyo, on the fifth day after she had last been seen at home, Mrs Carter of Nashville, Tennessee, had been on the thirty-five-foot *Dorado Queen* catching a five-hundred-sixty-eight-pound Pacific blue marlin.

Mrs Carter of Nashville. I decided to call Sam. I couldn't find his card in my Rolodex. I knew I had one at home.

I raced to the front office. Martha and Lee had clients at their desks. I went to Anna. 'Anna,' I said in an urgent almost whisper, 'do you have Detective Davis' card? I need his phone number, quick.'

Anna looked startled but flipped through her card file and found it.

'Thanks.'

I went to the back office and called. I got his voicemail and wanted to throw something. I left a message. 'Sam, I found something you need to know about. Call me at work as soon as you can.'

I couldn't work the rest of the afternoon. I printed out the blogs from the website and forwarded the site to Sam and to my home computer email address. I wrote an email to the charter service but deleted it without sending it.

I tried the main police department number, the number to call if you can live without calling 911, as the billboards say, and was immediately transferred to Sam's voicemail. I started to call Philip Carter but decided to wait until I had talked to Sam. At five, I tried calling Sam again. This time I left the message that I was leaving for home and to call my cell.

I was lucky not to have a wreck on the way home. Some days you survive Nashville traffic by grace. No message from Sam. I called again. New message: 'Sam, I'm home. Please call me as soon as you can.'

I tried his home. Julie answered. 'No, ma'am, he's not home yet. When he gets home or if he calls, I'll tell him to call you. He has your number, right?'

It was another long hour before he called. 'Something up?'

'Yes. Are you at a computer? I've got to show you something.'

'No, I'm in the car. I'm actually not far from you. I'll just come by, if that's OK.'

'Sure.'

'See you in a couple of minutes.' He hung up. In less than ten minutes, he was at my door.

SIXTEEN

'The airline said she was on the plane.' Sam was holding the printout I'd made from the fishing charter's online blog and shaking his head as he disconnected his mobile phone. 'Looks like she went to Mexico and went fishing. Had a good day, too. Five hundred sixty-eight pounds.' He looked up. 'Thanks. Have you told Carter or the Thompsons?'

'No. I wanted to show you first. You can tell them.'

'Yeah, OK. I think I'll call the charter company first to confirm everything.' A slight frown creased his face.

'This means something happened to her there, doesn't it?'

Sam shrugged. 'All it really means is that it's not my problem. Whether something's happened to her or she's just takin' a few days alone or whether she's tryin' to disappear, it's happenin' in Mexico, not Nashville. Until somebody hears from her or finds her, we still don't know if she's acting on her own free will or not. Nothing criminal in droppin' out of sight for a while. You've got child support issues, of course, but millions of parents take off every year. More often it's fathers than mothers, but you'd be surprised. More mothers than you'd think.'

'I don't believe it.'

He raised his hands, palms out. He'd learned not to argue with friends and family who couldn't believe it. Not my boy, not my husband, not my wife. Not my friend. 'I'm not sayin' that's what happened. She could very well have meant to call when she got back to the spa after that fishing trip and didn't make it back. That's not a very good option either.'

'What now?'

'I'll confirm this, let the family know, get in touch with the police down there. It's out of my jurisdiction, out of my hands.'

'Then what?'

'It depends. Without more to go on, I doubt if the police in Mexico are going to get too excited about it. They're gonna figure some Anglo broad decided to lose herself. If I were the Thompsons and had the money for it, I'd send a private investigator, which is what they're planning anyway. I guess this lets Carter off the hook.'

'Yeah, except that he still doesn't know if his wife is dead or alive.'

'Yeah, well, there is that. Look, Campbell, people do crazy things, even people you think you know. I'm sorry, but I hear it every day. And nobody wants to believe it.'

'I guess.'

'You got a phone number for this place?' I pointed to the number on the printout of the blog. 'OK, thanks. I'll let you know what happens.'

'Thanks.' I was glum. I'd been so excited to find something, some information finally. Now it didn't look like it helped very much.

'Hey. You did good work here.' Sam put his hand under my chin and tilted my head up so I had to look into those blue eyes. 'This family needs answers, and you've helped them start to find them. That's a good thing.'

I nodded. How come it didn't feel good?

SEVENTEEN

February is a dangerous time for me. That's why I understood Bitsy heading for the tropics. It's gray and mostly rainy in Nashville with just enough warm, sunny days thrown in to tease you. A high pressure front will move in from the west, its winds blowing huge, clockwise circles. It moves in to blast Tennessee with Minnesota winds, cold, arctic winds. Then, especially when the center moves right across us, as it goes past, those winds keep circling, stretching, warming, basking in the Caribbean sun, and they blow north again, warm from the Gulf of Mexico. One day it will be bitterly cold; the next I'll step outside to the teasing, false, seductive warmth of spring, and I can smell the ocean air. I can smell the ocean, and I want to be on it or near it, anyway.

The wind changed the next day, and I could smell it.

It was mid-morning when I got the call from Philip Carter.

'Campbell?'

'Yes.'

'Philip Carter. I just wanted to thank you.'

'Oh, you're welcome. I mean . . .'

'I know. Who knows what to say? Good news, bad news.'

'I'm sorry.' I fumbled.

'No, no. It's OK. I just . . . Look, you found out more than any of us have so far. It's a place to start. Whatever, whatever is going on or . . . happened, we need to know. The kids need to know. I need to know. Thanks. I . . . I just wanted to say thanks.'

'Philip . . .'

'I know. I know. Look, if you hear anything more, of course, let us know. And we'll be sure you know whatever, whatever we find out. We're sending, that is, the Thompsons are sending a detective. Bitsy's dad's already talked to the Mexican consul and the State Department. I'd go myself, but I don't know if that's the best thing for the kids.'

'I'm still hoping for the best.' It sounded feeble even to me.
'Yeah, thanks. I'll be in touch.'
I felt so bad for the man.

EIGHTEEN

I got a sandwich for lunch at a place near my office in the Village that makes its own bread fresh every day. I nodded to a few people I knew, people who worked in or around Hillsboro Village, but I wasn't very neighborly. I was thinking. How hard would it be to talk a friendly airline rep into a free ticket to Mexico? How soon could I get away, and how long could I stay without making everybody in the office mad? What could I possibly find out that a professional detective with an unlimited expense account couldn't? And did I really want to get messed up in this any more than I already was? I had vacation time coming. There weren't any crises hanging. It was February, for goodness sake. Where had I put my passport? I started making lists on my napkin.

Back across the street at the office, I put in a call to the rep with the airline I did the most group business with. If anybody would give me a ticket, she would. I left a message. It might take a day or so to hear from her if she was traveling.

I went out to the front office and waited until there weren't any clients in the office and everybody was off the phone at the same time.

'Anybody got any problems?'

Everybody looked up, surprised, suspicious, guarded.

'What do you mean?' Lee asked.

'I just mean, is everything under control?'

'I knew that jerk would call you,' groaned Martha. 'I'm working it out, Campbell. It won't be a problem. He's mad because the insurance company doesn't want to pay. He had to cancel his trip because his whole family was going to Disney World and his brother-in-law in the Navy's been transferred and the insurance company says that's a normal expectation of his job, which I think is a crock, but what can you do? Anyway, the tour company is going to refund everything except the air tickets, and we may be able to get the airline to refund that or waive the exchange fee for them to reschedule. Anyway, I'm working on it.'

I had to laugh. 'He hasn't called.'

'Oh.' Martha's voice was small.

Lee broke the silence. 'So what's this about?'

'I was just thinking of taking some time off if everything's under control. Nobody else has any time off scheduled for a while.'

'Kind of sudden,' Lee observed.

'Yeah, I'm not sure. I'm just thinking about it.'

'Where're you thinking about? Mexico?' Lee had it figured out.

'Maybe.'

'Alone?' It was Lee's parent voice.

'Maybe.'

'Then I've got a crisis. It requires your attention. Don't be stupid.'

'I won't be stupid.'

'Going to Mexico alone is stupid. Going looking for someone who either wants to disappear or has been murdered is stupid,' argued Lee. 'St Lucia would be smart. A cruise would be smart.'

I nodded and went back to my office.

NINETEEN

But when I melt in the sun

I watch for the birds flying high
Surfing the sky
Because when I see them

I wanna fly
Like an eagle takes to wing

Stick Anderson

By the time Gwen, my friendly airline rep, called back that afternoon, I had talked myself out of it. Lee was right. I couldn't even imagine what Sam would say. It was stupid; it was dangerous, and what I really needed was a genuine vacation.

'Got your message. Sure, you can have a ticket. Just don't tell anybody. I don't want to look easy. When do you want to go?'

I was easy. Whenever she could find the space.

'OK, you could go next Thursday. Just you or a companion, too?'

I hadn't thought about that. A companion? 'Could you hold it for two and let me get back to you tomorrow?'

'Yeah, sure. What about a return?'

'Three, four, five days later?'

I heard the keys of her computer clicking.

'There's plenty of return space Monday afternoon. How's that?'

'Great. Let me see if I can get the hotel lined up. Thanks, Gwen. I owe you.'

'That's my plan. Let me know.'

As I hung up, I was pulling my *Hotel & Travel Index* closer.

Spa Quetzalcoatl. A Place to Come Alive.

Three hours later, I had a drastically discounted two-bedroom suite reserved at the Spa Quetzalcoatl for Thursday through Sunday evening, checking out on Monday. I had talked to every client who might be expected to have questions about pending arrangements during that time. I had talked with two suppliers to extend deadlines that would fall on Monday. I had done everything except find a companion.

I called MaryNell and explained. 'Are you asking me to go? You're not asking me to go, are you? You're thinking about asking the detective, aren't you? You go, girl! I didn't think you had it in you. I mean, I'd like to go to Mexico; I'd like to go to a spa, but you go!'

'I don't know. I haven't propositioned anybody in a long time. Could you come?'

'No, not really, not with all the kids' activities. Nobody's propositioned anybody in a long time. Nobody uses that word anymore. What have you got to lose?'

'Self-respect? You know I don't handle rejection well.'

'Yes, I'll make sure I have a stockpile of anti-depressants. What's the worst that can happen?'

'He'll say no, run like the wind, I'll never see him again, and I still won't know what happened to Bitsy?'

'Exactly. Then I'll have to make all kinds of arrangements, and you'll have to take me to Mexico. Hurry up and call him. If I'm getting off work next week, I've got to get started. Plus I've got to get things situated at home.'

'Yeah, thanks for the encouragement.'

I took a deep breath. I dialed half the number, chickened out, hung up, breathed again – yoga breathing, inhale slowly, hold, exhale slowly – and dialed the whole number this time. Voicemail. I managed to croak my name and number and hung up. It was five thirty. I went home.

TWENTY

When I got home, there was a message from Mark. He had called from work and left the *Tennessean*'s number.

'City. Mark Allen,' he answered when I called.

'This is Campbell. You called?'

'Yeah. I heard something today about your friend, Bitsy. Or, actually, about the husband.'

'Oh, yeah?'

'Yep. Seems there's been some talk that Philip was a little too appreciative of the talents of the current au pair, an Irish national, who is, by Tennessee law, underage. Seventeen.'

'Where's the talk coming from?'

'Bitsy's friends, apparently, other mothers who have children in the same school. You know, sitting around at soccer practice, decorating for a school thing. Women talk.'

'Oh, women talk. I've heard that. Is that all?'

'Not quite. Seems the au pair is taking community college courses, and some of her school friends talk, too.'

'What does the au pair say? Maureen?' I had met her.

I heard Mark flipping pages.

'Right. Maureen Kennedy. Maureen isn't talking. The children are at the grandparents' house right now, and Maureen is staying there with them. Maureen may feel that she would be less welcome if the Thompsons think she's been having an affair with their missing daughter's husband. Maureen, by the way, is very attractive. Not that I've noticed over the years that that matters much. Ugly people have affairs, too.'

'Yeah, I've met Maureen. Lots of long, auburn hair. She's beautiful. People will talk, you know.'

'Yeah, and that may be all it is. She may have talked to her friends about what a hunk her employer is, may have bragged and exaggerated a little. Now, with everything in the news,

people start remembering things. Things that might have
happened or might not have. There's really nothing for us to
print yet. It's just gossip, so far, but it's coming from different
sources. Thought you'd want to know.'

'I do. Yeah. Thanks.'

TWENTY-ONE

I
t was late when Sam called. The news was off. I had given
up. I had called my neighbors, the Morgans, and told them
I might be planning a trip soon. Could they keep an eye
on things for me, pick up my mail? I had watched Stephen
Colbert's monologue and decided to take a bath. I was sure
Sam knew why I was calling and had decided to avoid me.
How can I have enough self-confidence to run a successful
business and not be able to offer a man a relatively free trip
to Mexico without breaking into a cold sweat? I thought it
was MaryNell when the phone rang.

'Campbell?'

'Sam! Hi.' I sat up too fast and splashed water everywhere.

'Are you doing OK? I had a message that you called.'

'Yeah, yeah, I did. Uh . . . Well, the thing is, I've decided
to go to Mexico.' Silence. 'I've got a free ticket and a room;
actually I have two free tickets if I want them, and it's a
suite, two bedrooms, at the Spa Quetzalcoatl. I'm gonna go.'
I realized I was talking too fast. 'What can it hurt? I'll go
see the charter people, talk to the staff at the hotel, have a
massage or two, some great meals. And, you know, since
I've got two tickets and this huge suite, well, you can go,
too, if you want to.' I stopped when I had to take a breath.

He didn't say anything for a second, a minute, seemed like
an hour. 'Ah, I don't know . . .'

'I understand. I just thought I'd ask. No problem.' I was
backing off as fast as I could.

'Wait a second.' He sounded amused, and as much as I
feared rejection, I hated being laughed at more. 'I didn't say

no; I said I didn't know. It's not our jurisdiction, of course, it's not even really our case yet. No body. It still could be nothing but a woman who decided to take off, especially since she went fishing. When are you going?'

'Next Thursday. Coming back the following Monday.'

I could hear him thinking. I couldn't tell what he was thinking, but I could hear it.

'I'll have to talk to the captain. I'm due time off, that's no problem, but I can't go down there and start nosing around without his OK.'

'Of course.'

'And Julie. I'll have to see about Julie, see if she can stay with her mom or a friend.'

'Of course.' I hesitated. 'She and my friend MaryNell's daughter are friends. I'm sure she could stay there.' Was that a mistake? Was I trying too hard? 'Look, you do what you want to. Just let me know.'

'When?'

'When what?'

'When do I need to let you know?'

'I don't know. Tomorrow? Day after? I need to let the airline rep know for sure.'

'If I can't work it out, you don't have any business going down there, you know that.'

'Excuse me? I have traveled without police protection, you know, without a man, even by myself. I'm a travel agent. It's what I do.'

'Looking for somebody who either wants to disappear or might have been murdered? People who kill people are dangerous. That's what *I* do, and I know it can get you hurt.'

'I'm just going to a spa. I'm not sneaking off. People will know where I am. I'll be fine.'

'Unless something did happen to her, and you're looking in the right place. Look, I'm not trying to make you mad or patronize you. Let me do some checking. I'll try to let you know tomorrow.'

'OK. Fine.'

By then the water was cold, and I looked like a large, pale raisin.

TWENTY-TWO

B y the next day, I was trying to get a realistic perspective on this whole trip. I probably wasn't going to find Bitsy and bring her home to an ecstatic and grateful family. I probably wasn't going to prove what had happened to her and return with some criminal in tow to make sure justice was served and Bitsy's suffering (that's as far as I would go, even to myself. I believe enough in visualization that I didn't want to imagine the worst) was avenged. I probably wasn't going to impress the veteran detective that I could do his job better than he and the combined police forces of Mexico and the United States of America. And I probably wasn't going to come back from Mexico with a usually tired, mostly cynical, middle-aged, single father detective madly in love with me. That little reality check session helped. Took some of the pressure off.

What could I realistically hope to accomplish? Get a little sun, see a part of Mexico I'd never been to before. Fish for marlin. Have a really good massage and some really good food. Not a total loss. Fish for a little information. I could at least show the Zihuatanejo Fishing Charters people Bitsy's photograph and make sure she was the one who had caught the five-hundred-sixty-eight-pound Pacific blue marlin. Maybe I could get addresses for the others who had been on the *Dorado Queen* with Bitsy that day. Then I could contact them and see what they remembered from the trip, what Bitsy might have mentioned about her plans for that night, the next day, her return home, the rest of her life.

I could wander in the shops and show her photograph around, talk to the Spa Quetzalcoatl staff, find out if they remembered anything. And I might have fun with the detective, might see some of the stress wrinkles smooth from his face, might actually enjoy spending some time with him.

And, if not, that might be the most important thing of all to learn.

With my mind temporarily straight, I decided I needed to let Bitsy's family know what I was doing. I called the Thompsons, but no answer. I left my name and number in response to the answering machine's request, but I didn't say any more. It didn't seem like the kind of message to leave on a machine. I tried Philip's number, Bitsy's number. Another answering machine.

'Hello. This is Philip Carter.' He gave the day and date. 'I'm at home today, in and around the house. Please leave a message.'

His voice had an anxiety, a desperation even, the sound of a man who wanted to know something, anything. I decided to drive out there. It wouldn't take long, and it was late enough for lunch anyway. Lee looked disapproving when I told him. I ignored the look.

TWENTY-THREE

In the soft, summer night

I touch the blue velvet sky
Close as you are to me
And warming me in the moon's light
I feel you beside me
Touching my skin
You're home, and you're safe
The one I come home to

Stick Anderson

I turned off Hillsboro Road onto a street where the lots were suddenly wooded. It was hard to believe this area was so close to the noise and traffic of Green Hills. I made another turn. Houses were set farther back from the street, shielded by woods. This was not an area where neighbors would wave from front porches or know each other's business.

I turned at the Carters' mailbox and wound up the serpentine drive. The street disappeared from view almost instantly. I got a whiff of wood smoke, leaves and brush burning, I supposed. I could see smoke ahead. Then I climbed around another curve and saw the house. It was brick and stone, looking for all the world as if it had been there for generations or had been transported magically from the French countryside, the brick rounded and softened with age. Old brick. The most expensive kind.

There was a fire in an open space a safe distance from the house. Was that legal, I wondered. Philip stood beside the fire, wearing a disposable mask with a hose lying ready beside him on the ground. Water ran down the hill. Philip turned as I got out of the car and closed the door. I saw his face change;

anticipation turned to disappointment, then recognition followed by a tired, closed politeness on his face.

'Hello!' He pulled the mask down off his face, but his attention was divided between me and the fire.

'Hi. I see you're busy. I don't want to interrupt,' I apologized.

'No, no. I won't ask you in, because I don't want this fire to get out of hand, but I'm glad to see you. It's just that . . . It's stupid, I know, but every time I hear a car, I think just for a second that she's home.'

'I'm sorry.'

He shrugged, smiled half a smile and nodded. 'I shouldn't really be doing this, burning these leaves and trash, but I had to do something. And I feel like I have to stay home, have to be here in case there's news.'

I nodded and looked, as people always do, at the fire. Leaves. This lot would have plenty of them. Technically, it's against the law to burn in Nashville without a permit, but, with so many leaves falling, lots of people do it anyway. Nobody seems to get too upset unless the weather's dry. If it is, there are warnings in the newspaper and on the news about the danger of fire. The recent soaking rain probably made Philip's little brush fire relatively safe. Small branches, long dead and dry, fallen in now-forgotten winter storms, were piled with leaves. I could see some two-by-fours underneath.

Philip turned to pick up some more small branches and tossed them on the fire. 'We were just starting this remodeling when she left. I told the construction crew to stop where they were when Bitsy's parents and I decided something was wrong. Except for the bath. The bath was already done except for painting it. They left their scrap lumber out here. I thought I could at least clean that up. Bitsy would hate the yard being trashy.' He took a deep breath and looked away.

I nodded again. There didn't seem to be anything to say.

I took a deep breath of my own and plunged in. 'Philip, I'm going to Mexico.'

He looked up, surprised. 'You?' Then, recovering, 'When?'

'Next Thursday.'

It was his turn to nod. 'I wish I could go with you. At least, it would be something.'

'I don't know that it will accomplish anything, Philip, but, I was talking to the people at the spa, and I got a free ticket, and I just thought, what can it hurt?'

He laughed, short and cynical, not a pleasant sound. 'Nothing, I hope.' He looked in my eyes. 'Please be careful. I don't want to think anything has happened to Bitsy, but I can't believe she wouldn't be home now if it hadn't. Don't put yourself at risk.' He poked at the fire with a stick. 'Do you really think it's safe to go?'

'I'm not going alone,' I said. Philip nodded again. 'I will be careful,' I continued. 'I'll talk to some people, show Bitsy's picture around. Oh, that reminds me. Do you have a couple of photographs I could make some prints of to take with me, to show people?'

Philip looked away, thinking, then back at me. 'Of course. They're in the house.' He looked calculatingly at the fire. 'I think it should be OK for a few minutes. Come inside.'

Philip led the way around back. The smoky smell was oddly stronger there. Bitsy's studio sat back from the house in a small separate building. It looked old, too, although I knew the house and studio had been built less than ten years before. Except for the skylights visible on the roof, the studio had the appearance of an out-building on the grounds of a French country chateau. Philip's gaze followed mine.

'I haven't been able to go into her studio since she left. It's so much a part of Bitsy. I think she was working on something the day before she left, actually.'

Through the large, paned windows I could see an easel and working tables, the big stone sink against the far wall. I'd been inside Bitsy's studio a couple of times. One day I'd brought a canvas and spent the afternoon painting while she glazed some pottery. One piece was the vase she had given me, the one with holly and evergreen branches in it at my house right now. I knew there would be trays of paints, some for canvas, some for clay and pottery, all neatly organized. There would be glazes for the pottery and varnishes for the paintings, photographs and sketches of ideas stuck around. Brushes would be separated, too, for pottery or for canvas. Canvases, waiting for inspiration or a commission, would be stacked vertically against the wall.

On the shelves, clay would be stored in airtight containers, chemicals to add to the clays for certain properties, bone ash for transparency, petalite to decrease shock from the huge changes in temperature, fluorspar for glazes. Bitsy was passionate about her art. Many of these chemicals could be poisonous, a danger if you forgot to wash your hands well before touching your eye or picking up a cookie. Others, like the fluorspar, were toxic during the firing process. Opening the kiln too soon could let toxic fumes escape into the studio. Pottery isn't for sissies, and Bitsy wasn't just a rich, spoiled ex-debutante. She understood the chemistry and had warned me about the dangers that day.

Beyond the work tables would be the kiln, big enough for large pots, set on firebricks to allow air circulation and protect the floor from the intense heat. Bitsy was very deliberate, choosing clays for the specific properties she wanted in a piece, adding chemicals to manipulate texture or color. I could remember Bitsy in there, imagine Bitsy in there, working, paint smeared on her face and clothes, about to notice us and come to the door.

I understood why Philip couldn't go in there. It was painful just to look at, knowing Bitsy wasn't there, might never come back to finish the last piece.

When I had worked in the studio with Bitsy a few times, I had mostly painted and glazed pre-cast pieces of greenware, several tiles for trivets, a pitcher or two, some small platters. Bitsy, though, ordered clay from specific locales known for certain characteristics and worked with it, in it, kneading and shaping. She'd throw a lump of clay on her wheel and spin it, dipping her hands in water to keep the clay malleable, shaping it, smoothing it. It looked to me like she was destroying what she'd started, but she kept on until it was something entirely new. Something I couldn't have imagined when she'd started.

Then she'd paint or glaze it. We'd put our work into the big kiln, my feeble little tiles and her creation. She'd set the kiln for 2000, 2400 degrees, turn on the timer, and we'd leave our work for the merciless heat to finish. The next day, after the kiln had slowly cooled, she'd open it up and call to tell me what we had, whether something had broken in the kiln, if the glazes had turned out to be the colors we'd hoped, whether it had all worked. The colors changed in the kiln, partly depending on what else was in the kiln, so it wasn't always entirely predictable. I hoped I'd be doing that again, playing while Bitsy worked, waiting for her call to tell me about the reds, the tricky reds.

The last time I had been in the studio, Maureen, the au pair, had been there with the children. Thompson had been painting a mug with sports designs and the colors and names of his favorite teams. Rachel had been painting flowers and vines on a tiny doll tea set.

Maureen had chosen a teapot that sat on its own mug, painting red stripes and a blue field around stars, an American tea set, she said, to send to her mum in Doolin, her tiny hometown on the west coast of Ireland. We had all laughed all afternoon. The next day, they had all come by the office to bring my piece, a platter for a friend's birthday, and show off theirs. Maureen had seemed like part of the family, a favorite niece, maybe. Surely Bitsy's disappearance didn't have anything to do with Maureen.

Philip opened the back door of the main house and held it open for me. We went in through a small entrance hall, a mud room, it was probably called on the plans, although it was spotless except for a small trail of gray dust leading to the door that I noticed as we stepped on it and scattered it. Ashes tramped in from the fire? I wiped my shoes to be sure I didn't track in any.

A wooden bench on one side had boots and gardening shoes underneath. A couple of caps and a straw hat hung on hooks above it. A large sink was against the opposite wall with herbs in flower pots on the counter beside it. An open door led into the kitchen.

'Wait here. I'll find the photographs. I know right where they are. I had to get some for the police and the news media.'

I looked around. I'd been here before, though not often.

Like everything else about Bitsy's house, the design was good, and the space was comfortable. There was a skylight, and windows looked over a flower garden, now brown and dormant, to the woods beyond. The kitchen floor was slate, and the countertops were granite, so there was a warm, organic feel. There were two ovens, a warming drawer, an industrial size refrigerator. Stools surrounded an island in the center of the workspace. It was a kitchen to use.

A painting of Bitsy's hung on one wall. It was of the children leaning over the edge of a pond, playing in the ripples with their fingers, their images reflected and distorted in the water.

Philip returned with two photographs. One was a print of the photo I had seen in the newspaper and on the news, Bitsy smiling from behind television news anchors for weeks. The other was a snapshot, one that I didn't think looked especially like Bitsy, but it was good to have two different shots. This one showed Bitsy full-length, in jeans and a sweater, walking with the kids. A hat shaded her face, and the most prominent feature was Bitsy's blonde hair, swinging in the sun.

TWENTY-FOUR

My next stop was the Thompsons' house. Not far away, also in Belle Meade, it was the house where Bitsy had grown up. It was huge, built of stone, with a lawn you could eat off. A small exaggeration, maybe, but everything was carefully groomed, not a blade of grass out of line or shooting up above its place. A pea gravel drive circled the lawn.

I stopped in front of the door. It certainly was imposing. What would it be like to be a child in a place like this? Thompson opened the door and looked lost. Maureen was right behind him, about to scold and pull him inside until she recognized me.

'Miss Hale,' she called with relief in her soft Irish tongue. 'There've been so many people, reporters and such. It's a terror, it is. The children want to play outside, of course, but we're afraid they'll be bothered. Come in, do.'

Maureen was pretty, no doubt about it. Her long auburn hair and green eyes gave her a delicate look totally unlike Bitsy's outdoorsy blonde strength. Perhaps it was also the fact of her being a young girl, half a world away from her home, but she always seemed a little shy, quiet, more at home playing with the children than talking with adults.

'Hi, Maureen. Hey, Thompson, how ya doin'?'

He hung his head. 'OK. Do you know where my mommy is, Miss Campbell?'

I knelt in front of him. 'I don't, Thompson. I'm sorry. I wish I did. I know one thing, though. Wherever she is, your mom loves you. I know that.'

He nodded, polite, but unconsoled. I couldn't blame him.

'Are your grandparents home?'

He nodded, dismissing me since I didn't have the answer to the only question that mattered.

Maureen spoke then. 'Mrs Thompson is inside, Miss Hale. Will you come in, then? Mr Thompson is at work, but the missus is here. I'll tell her you've come. Come along, then, Tommy.'

Thompson stuck his hand in Maureen's and let himself be led in the door.

I had met Bitsy's parents, but the friendship between Bitsy and me didn't extend to them. Mrs Thompson was gracious, always gracious. She would be pleasant and do whatever she could to make me feel at ease. It was her nature, her training, her upbringing. It didn't mean she liked me.

With Thompson still clinging to her hand, Maureen led me across the slate entry and down a long hall to a bright kitchen. There was a large sitting area off to the side separated from the working part of the kitchen by a glass-topped iron breakfast table. A dark chocolate brown woman of about sixty in a white uniform looked up from her work and nodded at me. Thompson ran to her.

'Carrie! This is my mommy's friend Campbell.' He grabbed her hand and pulled her to me.

'I'll just see if Mrs Thompson is busy,' Maureen said, leaving me to Carrie and Thompson.

Carrie wiped her hands as she let herself be dragged across the room. I put out my hand. 'I'm Campbell Hale.'

'Yes'm.' Carrie shook my hand. 'Carrie Johnson.'

'I see you have a buddy,' I said, nodding at Thompson.

'Yes'm.' She smiled indulgently. 'This one's a scamp, for sure. He knows how to get around me, I guess, just like his mamma.'

'Have you worked here long, then?' I asked.

'I reckon so.' Carrie nodded. 'Most of my life. I was working for Miss Bitsy's fam'ly before she was born.' She shook her head, suddenly sad. 'It's a bad thing. These chirren need their mamma.'

'Can we make some cookies, Carrie?' Thompson was obviously at home in this kitchen. 'Campbell will help.' And, cheerful as he was, he was obviously accustomed to people going along with his plans.

'Miss Campbell might have other things to do with her time, Mr Thompson. You ever think of that?'

'Well, she's not doing anything now,' he asserted reasonably, 'are you, Campbell?'

'I'm actually waiting to see your grandmother,' I answered, 'but I'll be glad to help while I wait.'

'Good.' He turned to the cook, problem solved. 'I knew she would help. I would like chocolate chip.'

'Let me see if I got the stuff.' Carrie was grinning as she turned to open a door that led into a pantry. Shelves inside were stocked with food staples.

Thompson turned to me with a loud, conspiratorial whisper. 'She always has chocolate chips for me.'

Carrie pulled out supplies as Thompson pulled a stool up to the island in the kitchen work area. I felt sure my help was superfluous, but I walked over.

'Are chocolate chips your favorite?' I asked.

'Yes. Rachel likes oatmeal best.'

'How's Rachel going to feel about us making chocolate chip?'

'Well, she didn't ask for oatmeal.' His argument was, again, perfectly reasonable. 'I asked,' he added smugly.

Carrie set out ingredients. She put two sticks of butter into a large bowl and handed it to Thompson along with a large spoon.

'I guess there's no news?' I asked her.

'No'm.' She sighed. 'Nothin' new.' She opened her mouth, then closed it sharply and looked at me significantly. 'Little pitchers.'

Thompson looked up from the butter he was creaming. 'She's talking about me, but I am not a pitcher; I'm a shortstop, and I do not have big ears.'

'Your ears look the perfect size to me,' I agreed.

Carrie shook her head as she turned to preheat the oven.

'Do you know how to make chocolate chip cookies?' Thompson asked me.

'Probably not as well as you and Carrie, but I've made them a few times.'

Thompson looked sideways at me and raised one eyebrow. He looked enough like his mother just then to make me catch my breath. 'Do you know how to make Bitsy-chip cookies?'

'I've never heard of Bitsy-chip cookies.'

'You gon' be givin' out all my secrets?' Carrie exclaimed in mock despair. 'How'm I gon' keep my job?'

Thompson laughed. 'I can tell her, but that doesn't mean she can make them taste like yours, Carrie. Momma says nobody can make Bitsy-chip cookies like yours even if they have the secret recipe. She says she can't even make 'em like you can, and they're her cookies. She made up the recipe.'

'Well, I do put a lot of love in 'em,' Carrie said, mollified.

'Yes, but Momma says she puts love in hers, too, but they still don't taste the same.'

'Yo' momma just lazy and want me to make 'em for her.'

Thompson laughed and creamed in the sugar, then added eggs, vanilla, flour, as Carrie handed him the ingredients with the precision of a surgical nurse.

He poured in chocolate chips, putting his shoulder behind his stirring as the batter thickened. 'Now comes the secret ingredient,' he whispered. 'Can you keep a secret?'

I nodded.

'Promise?'

I made an X across my heart. 'Cross my heart.'

'Well, actually, there are two secret ingredients,' he said. 'Carrie uses Mexican vanilla.' He stopped stirring and looked to make sure he had my full attention. 'It's the best kind.' He looked back to his work. 'I think maybe that's why Momma went to Mexico. To get some more vanilla to make cookies for me.'

I nodded solemnly.

'But this is what makes them Bitsy-chip cookies.' He held a square glass container out for my inspection. 'Butterscotch chips!'

'Butterscotch chips in chocolate chip cookies?'

Thompson nodded, pleased with his surprise. 'Yes, and wait until you taste them.' He poured in the chips, and he and Carrie set about scooping dough onto a parchment-covered cookie sheet.

Maureen came back into the kitchen then to tell me Mrs Thompson would see me. 'She's in the den, miss. I'll show you the way.'

I followed Maureen through a hallway, thinking that Maureen's attitude didn't seem to be that of an employee who had done away with her employer to marry – or whatever – the husband. I don't know what evidence I thought there would be of that in someone's walk or talk, but it didn't seem to be there in Maureen. No swagger, no attitude, no superiority, no sense of 'I know something you don't'. Was she afraid? Was she involved with Philip at all, and, if so, had it been her choice? This didn't seem the place to ask.

'Maureen.'

'Yes, miss?'

'Do you have free time? I mean, I know you're in school. Maybe an afternoon or evening? I'd like to take you to dinner, maybe talk about Bitsy a little. Would that be OK?'

Maureen stopped in front of me and turned around to face me. She was definitely afraid. The question was, why? 'I dunno, miss.'

The last thing I wanted to do was make her afraid of me. 'I'll tell you what. This is my card.' It disappeared quickly into a pocket. 'You call me when you have some time.'

She looked away, looking at once older and younger than

she had with Thompson on the driveway. Younger in that she looked terrified, older because there was no innocent sense in that face that things were right with the world.

'Yes, miss. Thank you.'

She opened a pair of deeply carved wooden doors to show me into a room in which Mrs Thompson looked completely out of place. The den was large and determinedly masculine, paneled in cherry, guarded by the heads of dead animals lining the room near the twelve-foot ceiling. There were deer and antelope, not roaming here, with glassy eyes silently watching. No chance of a discouraging word. There was a moose. A small, stuffed red fox guarded the fireplace. I wondered if the Thompsons had a dog or cat and if pets felt as nervous as I did in this room.

Mrs Thompson rose from her chair at the far side of the room. She was an attractive woman, had once been beautiful, but it wasn't just age that marked her face today. There was worry, of course, for her lost daughter, but something else, something that had been there a lot longer than her concern for Bitsy's disappearance, had given her a fragile, almost brittle look. She saw me looking at the trophies above us, and smiled apologetically.

'My husband's souvenirs. I often think it's a little grotesque to live with dead animals as decorations, but what can you do?'

I nodded and smiled. 'Mr Thompson must be an excellent hunter.'

'My husband hires excellent guides.'

So much for polite chitchat on the decor.

'I keep hoping to hear that you've heard from Bitsy.'

The gray in her face was even more noticeable. 'We've heard nothing. The police can't seem to find a trace. Your information from Mexico is the only positive news we've had. I should have written to thank you before now. And . . . Mr Thompson wants to thank you more substantially.'

Was she talking about paying me? Or paying me off?

'No, no. You don't need to thank me. I'm just glad we found something. That's really why I came today.'

'Of course, what can I do for you?'

I had the feeling that the two of us were in different conversations.

'I'm going to Mexico. I just wanted to let you know that, to ask you if there's anything specific you want me to do while I'm there, anyone in particular you want me to see?'

She looked alarmed. 'You're going to Mexico? Why? You mustn't do that!' She stopped and visibly calmed down. 'It may be very dangerous. We certainly wouldn't want you hurt, as well. And, besides, we've already sent a private detective. I don't want to offend you, but he is trained in this. What could you do that he can't?'

'Probably nothing,' I agreed. 'It was just a whim, really. I have some vacation time. I've never been there. I thought I'd go, ask around, show Bitsy's picture. It may not be any help, but what can it hurt? I'm not going alone. A detective is going with me, I think.'

Then, just for a moment, I saw real alarm on her face. For me? Surely not for fear of what I might find? Then she drew herself up.

'I feel sure Mr Thompson would like to talk with you before you go. When do you plan to leave?'

'Next Thursday.'

She looked away, out the window beyond the manicured lawn. 'Please be careful, Miss Hale. I wouldn't want to feel responsible for something happening to you as well.'

'I will.' What else could I say? She continued to stare out the window and didn't turn back to me. After an uncomfortable silence, I stood. 'I'd better be going then. I just wanted to let you know.'

Still turned away from me, she nodded. As I left the room, I had the sudden feeling that she was not insensitive to the intimidation factor in this room when she chose to meet me here. The deer and the antelope watched without blinking as I left.

Maureen was waiting for me in the hallway. Out of earshot? Although, what did it matter? What was there to hear?

'You'll be wantin' to say goodbye to Tommy, then, before you go. I'll show you back to the kitchen, will I?'

'Yes, of course. Thanks, Maureen.' I paused. 'Are you doing OK? This has to have been a shock to you, too.'

'Yes, miss, it has that. I surely didna expect anything like this. I mean, they warned me about the men, seems they often take a fancy to a young nanny in the house, so that wasna a problem, but this! I'm thinkin' Doolin's not sich a bad place t' be.'

'Was Mr Carter bothering you, then?'

'Ah, miss, I shouldna be sayin' anythin', and him half crazy with worry or grief. It was niver anythin' serious. Just flirtin', I'm sure. And with Mrs Carter . . . I shouldna be sayin' anythin' here at all.'

Suddenly she seemed to remember where she was, and that was the end of the conversation.

'Look, Maureen.' I pulled out another business card and handed it to her. 'If you think of anything or if you just need to talk to somebody, call me. All my numbers are there, and my email address.'

Again the instant disappearing act as my card was swept into a pocket. She nodded quickly. Mrs Thompson stepped out of the den into the hall just as we turned into the kitchen, and I thought Maureen seemed to be relieved to be out of the woman's sight.

The kitchen smelled of cookies and chocolate and, I believe Carrie must have been right, love.

Thompson looked up as we entered. 'Campbell! You're just in time. The first batch is out. Here.' He pointed to rows of cookies cooling on their parchment paper. 'Be careful. They're hot.'

I lifted a cookie carefully. He was right. It was hot, so soon out of the oven that it was soft and drooped in my hand as I lifted it to my mouth. Thompson waited expectantly. I didn't disappoint him. They were wonderful.

'Mmmm. Thompson, you were right to choose chocolate chip or, what did you call them, Bitsy-chip? This may be the best chocolate chip cookie I've ever tasted.'

Carrie looked on, accepting with accustomed modesty the accolade she knew she deserved.

'Yep,' Thompson agreed. 'They're the best. And when my mommy gets home we're going to make some together, me and mommy and Carrie.'

'That's right, you scamp,' Carrie agreed. 'Now you get on
and play. Let me clean up this kitchen and get your dinner done.'

I left a card with Carrie, too, and thanked her as she sent
me home with a paper plate of cookies. Maureen and
Thompson showed me to the door. As I got into my car, a
big Mercedes pulled up behind me on the circle drive. Everett
Harrison Thompson got out, and Maureen's fair skin paled
even further.

TWENTY-FIVE

'**M**iss Hale, I'm glad I caught you. My wife said you
had come by. Do you have a moment to come back
inside?'

Nothing about that question left any room for choice. But
I'd wanted to talk to him, so that was OK with me.

'Of course. How are you doing? I know this has been
agonizing.'

'Yes,' he said stiffly. My sympathy was apparently a
presumption, and it was not welcome.

He held the door as I went back in. I followed him back to
the den; Mrs Thompson was gone. He closed the den doors
behind us and walked over to a tray of bottles and a decanter.
'Would you like a drink, Miss Hale?' His hand hovered above
the bottles.

'No, thank you.'

He nodded, then reached for a bottle. Single malt.
Glenfiddich. The glass he poured it into was Waterford. He
drank it straight, no ice, no water. Then he looked at me.

'This room is impressive. All these are yours, of course?'

He nodded, looking around at the trophy heads. 'That buck
is my prize,' he said, nodding toward a majestic deer.
'Seventeen-point rack. One shot, two hundred eighty yards.
Never knew what hit him, never felt a thing.'

I nodded, not knowing what to say. My family weren't
hunters. I didn't know how to make conversation about it as

I could have on football or basketball, golf, politics, most any other topic.

'That one' – he gestured with his glass toward an antelope whose head, I realized, was at a different angle than the others on that wall – 'that one is not perfect somehow. I think the wound was a little high, and the taxidermist had to make some adjustments. It's a little off. A shame, really. That one cost me the most. Up in Montana. Expensive trip.' He shrugged, and I thought how difficult it would be to live in the house of this man and not be perfect. I shivered inside and thought I caught an understanding glance from the antelope. The moose came from Alaska.

He took another long drink from the glass and turned to me. 'My wife tells me you intend to go to Mexico.'

She must have called him, and he'd gotten here fast.

'Yes.' I wondered why I had ever thought coming here was a good idea.

He tapped his fingers on the glass. The antelope and I waited.

'What do you hope to accomplish?'

I repeated what I had told his wife. I was beginning to think a vacation in Maine sounded good. Didn't these people want Bitsy found?

'I know you want to help,' he said. 'My wife and I appreciate that, but, really, we've hired professional help. It would be very . . . unwise for you to go to Mexico yourself.'

I frowned. Was he offering advice, or did he not want me meddling? Was there a threat implied there? Or was he just being cautious, protective? After all, one woman had already disappeared.

'Thanks. I appreciate your concern. I've traveled a lot, you know. It's my work. I've even traveled in Mexico quite a bit. I know there are always risks, but I'm experienced and pretty prepared. I will be careful.'

He nodded, his eyes evaluating. He shrugged. 'Well. I'd rather you wouldn't go. And, frankly, I don't want anyone making things more difficult for the professional investigators. I'm sure you understand. This is too important. I'm afraid you may . . . muddy the waters, scare some people underground and make it harder for us to find out what's happened. I'm sorry to be so blunt, but, after all, this is my daughter.'

He didn't seem sorry. But how could I blame him? His only daughter was missing. He was pulling every string he could, and he could pull a lot of strings.

'I do understand. The last thing I'd want to do is make things harder for you and your family or interfere. I will be careful. I'll try very hard not to stumble around and upset things. Maybe your detective will already have found Bitsy before I go. I just think, particularly at the hotel, since I'm . . . in the business, sort of, people there may talk to me. I may pick up something. I'll be very careful.'

He nodded, unconvinced. 'Well, thank you for your time, Miss Hale.'

I knew when I was dismissed. I thanked him and left.

When I got into my car, two photographs of Bitsy were on the passenger seat. One was a print of the photograph from the paper, Bitsy smiling. The other was a family photo: Bitsy, Philip, Rachel and Thompson all happy and in red for Christmas. Someone wanted me to have pictures of Bitsy. Mrs Thompson with a change of heart? Carrie? Maureen?

TWENTY-SIX

I stopped at the end of Belle Meade Boulevard before pulling out onto Harding Road. I waited for the light to change, the bronze horses in the median beside me caught in perpetual play. I noticed Carrie, the Thompsons' maid, sitting in the bus stop shelter. There's always been a great bus service between Belle Meade and Nashville's predominantly black neighborhoods. The maids and the yardmen have to have some way to get to work every day. The city fathers have always seen to that.

I pushed the button to lower the passenger side window. 'Carrie!' I yelled. 'Can I give you a ride?'

'Miss Hale?' She walked over to the car and looked in, cautious in the gathering dusk.

'Yes. I'll be glad to take you home if you'd like.'

'Yes'm, if you don't mind. I'd appreciate that.' She opened the door and eased in, settling her shopping bag beside her. 'It's a chilly afternoon.'

'You're on your way home?'

'Yes'm.'

Carrie settled the shopping bag she carried on her lap and gave me general directions to her street.

'It must have been tough the last couple of weeks,' I said.

Carrie sighed. 'Yes'm. Those chirren are a pity. They loved they mother.'

I noticed the past tense. 'Loved? You think Bitsy's . . . dead?' I didn't want to say the word, but to talk in euphemisms like 'something's happened' seemed ridiculous. Of course, *something* had happened to her.

'If Miss Bitsy was alive, she would be with those chirren or they'd know why.' There was nothing for me to say. Her voice had absolute conviction. And I agreed with her.

We passed through the congested shopping area of Belle Meade, past Belle Meade Plaza, past what had once been the grand art deco Belle Meade Theater, where I had first seen Atlanta burning in *Gone with the Wind*, past St Thomas West Hospital and in toward downtown on West End.

'You work at Bitsy's, too, don't you? Did she say anything to you about this trip? I'm sorry. I know the police must have asked you every question imaginable.'

Carrie sniffed. 'Policeman just asked me was I there that day or the day after, and I wasn't. Ain't been back in that house since Bitsy disappeared.'

'Why?'

Carrie sniffed again, her disapproval obvious. 'I don't know why. Miss Bitsy would want her house kept neat whether she was there or away. Mr Philip just called to say I could take a break while Miss Bitsy did, said they'd pay me just the same, said Miss Bitsy thought I needed a little vacation, too. I asked what about the chirren, and he said the nanny would be there. Well, I knew that would not do, Mr Philip already makin' eyes at her, always makin' excuses to take somethin' to her room, offerin' to drive her places. I don't know that nothin' had happened yet, that chile looked too scared. But it was on Mr Philip's mind. That was plain to see. I just dropped a hint to Miz Thompson, and those chirren was over to her house in a minute, the nanny, too.'

'So had Bitsy mentioned the trip to you, asked you to help her get ready, pack, anything like that?'

'No, *ma'am*.' Carrie's emphasis on the 'ma'am' wasn't just out of respect; it intensified her denial. 'Miss Bitsy never said a word. Nobody asked me, but I don't think she went nowhere. That chile' – Bitsy would always be a child to this woman who had helped rear her, no matter how old she was – 'would no more have gone off to Mexico without makin' a list for me and goin' over it, than the man in the moon.'

I didn't tell her about the fishing report in Mexico. It didn't seem kind to try to diminish Bitsy in the eyes of a woman who'd cared for her since she was a child. Time enough to resolve those issues when Bitsy was found. Besides, I thought I'd learn more by listening than by arguing.

'What do you think happened?'

'I think Mr Philip knows more than he's tellin'. And Mr Everett, Bitsy's father, too. They was talkin' and spendin' a lot of time together right before Miss Bitsy disappeared. And Mr Everett don't seem near enough concerned about Miss Bitsy.'

'What do you mean?' I asked.

'Miz Thompson's near out of her mind, for all Mr Everett's told her not to talk to nobody. She don't say nothin', but she looks to be shrinkin' ev'ry day. It's like she's just gon' disappear. I'm worried about her. But Mr Everett just looks annoyed.'

'What's he like? In normal times, I mean?'

'He's not mean,' she said, thinking. 'He just acts like I'm invisible unless he wants somethin'.'

'How did you come to work for the Thompsons and Bitsy, too?'

'When Miss Bitsy and Mr Philip got married and set up housekeeping, Mr Everett just told me that I was to go to Miss Bitsy's two days a week.'

'Told you?'

'Yes'm.'

'Had he heard about the Emancipation Proclamation, do you think?'

Carrie smiled a small, tight smile. 'If he did, he don't let it bother him none.'

'Why do you stay?'

'Well, I didn't mind goin' to Miss Bitsy. I was glad. And it's a good job. Mr Everett gives me a nice little bonus at Christmastime. I'm used to their ways. It's a sight nicer workin' in a nice house on a quiet street than on your feet all day in a Walmart, except for the benefits and all. And Miss Bitsy. I've loved that sweet chile all her life. I'd miss her for sure.'

There didn't seem to be anything to say to that. We were both quiet for a while, thinking of the woman we both cared for. After a few minutes, I broke the silence. 'Are . . . were Bitsy and Philip happy, do you think?'

I thought Carrie wasn't going to answer, and I was afraid I'd gone too far, asked a question that was over the line, but Carrie seemed to accept me as one of the extended family of people who cared about Bitsy. 'You're not married, are you, Miss Campbell?'

'No. I've never been married.'

She nodded. 'When you been married a while – and when you get to be as old as I am, seen as much as I seen – you wonder what happy is exactly. Miss Bitsy was a person who decided to be happy. Didn't everything have to go her way for her to be happy.'

I didn't learn any more during the rest of the ride to the other West Nashville, the state streets or the Nations, as they're known, a little neighborhood off Charlotte where the streets are named for the fifty states, separated by very little distance but light years of status from nearby increasingly trendy Sylvan Park.

Carrie's house was the neatest on her block, a trim, neatly painted box in a well-cared-for yard with holly shrubs and mulched flower beds waiting for spring.

I was a bit disappointed as I pulled away. I had hoped

Bitsy had confided in her childhood housekeeper. I had hoped she would have an idea why Bitsy had left her family to go fishing in Mexico. And whom she'd gone with.

TWENTY-SEVEN

When I got home, there was no message from Sam, but he had called. His number was on my Caller ID. Didn't want to leave a message. Probably wanted to tell me in person that he wasn't going. I microwaved a frozen Lean Cuisine and made a list of things to do before I left. Sunscreen. I had to remember to get some sunscreen. By the time the phone rang, I had convinced myself that Sam didn't want to go, that he'd decided I was a pushy, aggressive woman and thought I was a nosy busybody. I steeled myself to get through it.

'Campbell?'

'Hi, Sam.' I waited, not planning to make this easy for him.

'OK. I've got it all worked out. I have years of comp time coming. The captain smirked, but he said OK. Told me to check in with the local police just to be polite. Said he'd call the chief he's talked with down there, let him know I'm coming, reassure him that I'm not trying to invade his turf.'

I didn't know what to say. I hadn't prepared myself for anything but rejection.

'Campbell?'

'That's great.'

'What do I need to do?'

'You have a passport, I hope?'

'Yep. I just have to find it.'

'Just pack and show up, then. I'll get you a copy of the itinerary. TSA pre-approval would be nice, but we don't have time.' I told him about Philip and the photographs, about Thompson and the Bitsy-chip cookies, about Everett Thompson's pets. He didn't approve of my asking, but he wanted to know what I'd learned.

When I hung up, I decided to reconsider my list. Why hadn't I gone to the Y three times a week like I'd promised myself? Maybe a new swimsuit.

TWENTY-EIGHT

I t really is a lot of trouble to travel at short notice. I had to make sure everything that could be foreseen was taken care of for clients with trips pending. I had to make sure Lee and the others in the office knew how to reach me about the things that couldn't be foreseen. I rescheduled a dental appointment. What a shame. I'd have to wait almost a month if I missed the one on Friday.

I had to make sure my neighbors would take in my mail and newspapers. I used to call and stop my paper delivery when I went out of town until I learned that they write your name and address up on a big board in the newspaper delivery center for anyone to see. Everyone knows if you stop your paper for five, seven days or so, you're out of town. Please rob me. I'd had a close enough brush with an intruder at my home when a friend turned murderer wanted to scare me. I asked Mr Morgan, the retired Navy Seal next door, to keep an eye on things for me.

I didn't see Sam. He was probably as busy as I was, making sure things were covered, making sure Julie was supervised. She was going to stay with Melissa. MaryNell told Sam that of course Julie could stay. She could have stayed with her mother, but Julie and Melissa would have the same school and ballgame schedule. Later MaryNell offered me her black spaghetti strap evening dress and insisted I name my first child for her. I hung up while she laughed. I emailed an itinerary to Sam, talked to him on the phone a couple of times. He was polite; I was polite. We didn't seem to know how to handle the idea of this trip. If once upon a time my motives had been mixed, I decided it was a waste. I might find some information about Bitsy in Mexico, might turn up a few leads for the Thompsons' investigator to follow up on, but the closer it got to time to leave, the more distant Sam and I seemed to be.

The night before our six thirty a.m. flight, he called. 'I'll pick you up in the morning.'

'There's no need,' I said. 'I can drive, leave my car in long-term parking.'

'I'll pick you up at five.' There were some advantages to living near the airport. 'If I'm going along to protect you, I don't want you wandering around in the dark and getting attacked before we leave Nashville.'

'I travel all the time, you know. I've read all the books; I even give talks on women traveling alone. Besides, you're not going along to protect me.'

'I'm not sure why I am going along, but I'll pick you up at five.'

It was too late to repack, or I might have taken out the black dress and the new swimsuit. This whole trip was a mistake. Why hadn't I listened to Lee and Philip Carter and Everett Thompson when they'd told me so?

TWENTY-NINE

Sam picked me up at five, and I was really glad he did. I'd been awake half the night packing, so I was asleep before the Fasten Seat Belt sign was off. I managed to rouse myself enough to have coffee and an unidentifiable pastry. Sam had a laptop out and seemed to be working, but I was too sleep-deprived to care. That's just great, I thought. He's a morning person. We didn't talk. I'm not good company when I haven't had enough sleep. And at six thirty, I've never had enough sleep.

By the time we deplaned in Houston, I looked like I'd slept in my makeup and clothes. I had. How did some people manage to look beautiful and intriguing when they traveled? I could never manage anything but wrinkled and disheveled. The black

knit dress I'd chosen for comfort seemed baggy and stretched
out in the wrong places after a couple of hours on the plane.
How did that happen? I'd just been sitting there. I hadn't
had enough room to move.

I had a pass to the executive lounge, so we spent our layover
in the relative luxury of wide leather chairs with unlimited
coffee, fruit and snacks. I began to wake up. I stretched, went
to the ladies' room to try to remake myself and returned to
find Sam plugged into a data port and frowning at his laptop
screen.

'You're awake,' he said, looking up as I sat down across
from him. 'I was beginning to think you'd been drugged by
a voodoo *obeah* and were doomed to roam the earth with the
undead.'

'Thanks. That's an appealing picture.' I wasn't that awake
yet. I gestured toward the laptop. 'You're working?'

He shrugged. 'Catching up on some reports. There's always
paperwork. But I just checked my email. Somebody turned in
your friend's day planner. I wish that had happened before we
left.' He looked mildly annoyed. 'The lab will have it for a
while anyway, but I'd like to see it.'

'Who turned it in? Where was it?'

'Guy from a church out in Donelson. They host Room in
the Inn once a week.' Sam referred to a program that a lot of
Nashville churches participate in. Most every winter night, a
different church hosts some of Nashville's homeless for the
night. Members provide supper; there's a place to take a shower
and a warm, dry place to sleep. Most churches provide clean
clothes, too, maybe new winter gloves, hats, even coats. The
program runs from October through March, when Nashville
nights can be cold and wet and mean.

'Which one?' I asked. 'Which church?'

He named one that I passed every day, but I didn't know
anyone who went there.

So how did a homeless man find the day planner of a woman
who lived in Belle Meade in Donelson?

Sam went on with the story, summarizing what was on his
screen. 'He was sittin' talkin' to a guy who'd come in from
the Mission, and the guy showed it to him. He was real proud

of it. The minister recognized the name, said he had to trade the guy the Titans sweatshirt he was wearing and ten dollars for it. He got the guy's name, but we may never find him.' Sam looked up. 'The minister tried to get him to tell where he'd found it, but the guy was cagey, said he'd found it beside a dumpster near the airport. The minister said he'd recognize him, and the people who are in the Room in the Inn program have to register with the Mission downtown; lots of them go back to the same churches every week. We may be able to track him down. The thing will be getting him to show us where he found it – if he remembers.'

'What will it tell you?' I asked.

'I don't know. Maybe not much. It might tell us something about Bitsy's trip, who she saw in the last few days before she left, what she had planned.'

'Well, that's good, isn't it?'

'Maybe.' Sam didn't seem convinced. He looked up at me again. 'Healthy people usually have their planners with them, or at home or in the car, maybe at the office. Not behind a dumpster.'

'Oh.' I realized what he meant. This might give us good information, but it wasn't good for Bitsy that the indispensable tool she used to organize her life was the trophy of a man who scavenged waste bins for a living. 'Coach.' I suddenly and irrelevantly remembered. Sam looked startled. 'Her day planner was Coach,' I explained. It was expensive, good leather. I shrugged. 'I don't know. That just hit me.' I could see Bitsy sitting beside my desk, scribbling the details of a trip, noting when she should pick up the documents, what she should take, what she had to do first. The Coach day planner was not something she'd be careless with.

From that point on, Sam was itchy, impatient. This trip might be a wild goose chase, but there were real leads at home, and he wasn't there to follow them. He had left thinking nothing was happening in the case. Maybe he could stir something up in Mexico. But now things had changed. Things were happening in Nashville without him.

Sam emailed furiously, then chomped on carrot sticks while he waited for replies and our flight. The day planner showed obvious signs of having been out in Nashville weather, but not as much as the investigator writing to Sam would have expected. It was thick, expensive, well-tanned leather, of course. That helped. But I was remembering that day or two of solid rain. Wouldn't any writing be obliterated after that? The leather cording at the edges showed wear; all gloss was gone from the surface, but a lot of the pages were clearly legible, he wrote. The investigator offered to scan the pages and email them to Sam if the lab released them before we returned.

Sam declined. 'That's all we need,' he muttered. 'Everybody handling the thing page by page. But if he can get photos from the lab, maybe he can email scans of those.'

'What can the lab find after all this time, all that time out in the rain and cold?' I asked when he looked up from his laptop.

'Probably nothing.' Sam was not optimistic. 'We'll find the vagrant's fingerprints, maybe some from a dozen others we'll never identify, the minister's, although he was apparently very careful with it after he realized what he had. If the prints of anybody in the family are on it, we'd expect that. It wouldn't mean anything.' He shook his head. 'It would just be pure, blind luck if anything turns up from this, but it's something. It's the first concrete thing we've found.'

What about Bitsy on the fishing boat, I wanted to ask. What about that? But it seemed a little petty, so I kept quiet.

'Wouldn't any prints be ruined by the weather?' I asked instead.

Again Sam shrugged. 'Yeah, maybe. You never know. It might, of course, not have been out in the weather this whole time. Somebody may have had it, just planted it behind the dumpster in the last few days. They'll probably test it with superglue.'

I looked blank, envisioning a mess of superglue all over the once beautiful leather.

'They put an object in an air-tight chamber, heat superglue below the item until the glue vaporizes. The glue fumes adhere to latent prints. Much better than dust,' he said with emphasis. 'The thing is, there'll probably be too many prints for it to be useful.'

'Superglue.'

'Yeah.' He smiled for the first time since he'd read the email. 'Shipping staff in a superglue factory discovered it by accident. They noticed that their fingerprints would be all over outgoing packages even when their hands were clean. Turned out it was the fumes.'

I grimaced. 'Makes you hate to think about their lungs.'

Sam nodded.

The disembodied voice of the receptionist at the entrance to the lounge announced our flight, and Sam closed his laptop with obvious reluctance. We gathered our carry-ons and headed for the gate and for the rest of a trip that both of us hoped wouldn't be a waste.

THIRTY

I stayed awake for the second leg, but Sam and I still didn't talk much. He seemed to be thinking. I guess I was, too. At one point, somewhere over Arizona, I turned to him. 'How long had he had it?' I asked.

'What? Who?'

'How long had the homeless man had the day planner?'

'I don't know. Good question.'

Bitsy had been gone for weeks. 'How likely is it that a day planner that was left in a dumpster nearly a month ago would have just been found this week?'

'Not very,' he answered.

'Can you find out? When the man found it, I mean?'

'Maybe. If we can find the man again. And if he's been sober enough to remember. We can talk to the minister, at least. I'll call and get somebody on it when we land.'

For the rest of the flight, we both had to be content with that.

At the Customs counter in the Ixtapa terminal, Sam pulled a folded letter from his inside jacket pocket and handed it, with his opened passport, to the inspector.

The inspector looked up sharply. 'Wait a moment, *por favor*, *Señor* Davis.' He picked up a phone and spoke a few sharp words, then turned back to us. Sam set the black bag he had checked on the counter and unlocked it. The inspector put his hand out to stop Sam. '*Uno momento, por favor.*' His tone allowed no debate.

Another official approached, flanked by two security guards. The official's right hand rested on his holstered pistol; the two guards carried rifles. I was beginning to get nervous. I tried to look innocent. The heat was oppressive after leaving Nashville in winter. The black dress felt like it was sticking to me in all the most unattractive places.

Without a word, the Customs inspector handed Sam's passport and letter to the new official. He read the letter slowly, then carefully inspected Sam's passport and his face. Sam was impassive. He stared into my face, and I had no idea how to react. Moving slowly and deliberately, he pulled his MNPD identification out and handed it to the official. The guards' eyes followed his hands.

Finally the official spoke. 'May I see your weapon, *Señor* Davis? It is in this bag?' He indicated the bag Sam had started to open.

Two more armed guards showed up behind the inspector.

'Yes, sir,' Sam replied. 'Would you like me to get it out?'

'*Gracias, Señor* Davis, but I think not. I will open your bag, if you do not mind.' Sam nodded. The official opened the bag and removed the locked case. Sam offered the key. The official took it, unlocked the case and inspected Sam's gun. He checked to make sure it wasn't loaded, replaced it in the case, relocked the case and looked up.

'I trust you will have no need of this on your visit, *señor.*'

'I feel sure that I won't, sir.'

'*Sí.* Welcome to Mexico, *Señor* Davis. Enjoy your visit.'

'Thank you.'

'And you, *señorita.*' I was dismissed. I realized I was sweating, and not only from the heat. I felt the eyes of every uniformed official and guard on me all the way out of the terminal.

Outside, the car from Spa Quetzalcoatl was waiting for us,

identifiable by the discreet logo of the spa on the side of the large black Mercedes. Its uniformed driver stood beside it holding a sign with my last name. I waved as we approached him.

'*Señorita* Hale?'

'Yes.' I smiled. There is no greater luxury than a car to meet you at a strange airport.

'Welcome to Mexico, *señorita, señor.*'

'Thank you.'

'May I take your luggage, *por favor?*'

He held the rear door as we climbed in, then loaded our bags into the trunk.

THIRTY-ONE

The ride to the spa was uneventful. The driver's name was Jésus. I asked him to take us by Zihuatanejo Fishing Charters before we went to the spa, but no one was there. A note on the door gave the phone number. Jésus speculated that they were out fishing this time of day and assured me the concierge would arrange a day of fishing for me and the *señor.*

As we drove into the mountains, heat shimmered off the asphalt, an endless mirage ahead of us. Jésus did not remember Bitsy. He also didn't speak much English, just enough to tell us he couldn't help us. We didn't speak much Spanish. Maybe this trip really was a waste.

'Ah, *sí, Señora* Carter. *Sí.* No, I do not know.'

'Have you heard anyone else talking about her? Does anyone at the spa have any idea what might have happened to her?'

'No, *señorita.* I do not know.' He made the sign of the cross. 'No one knows, but . . . *banditos?*' He shrugged. 'It is not wise to go alone.' He had my attention. Observation or warning?

I showed Bitsy's picture to Jésus. '*Bonita, sí,* but I do not know.'

Sam had leaned back against the cushioned side of the Mercedes and seemed to be asleep. So far, he was no help at all. Jésus talked about the spa and the region as we rose higher into the mountains, his mixed Spanish and English nearly incomprehensible in either language.

I made notes as I asked Jésus the names of the other drivers. Who might have been around the spa the day Bitsy arrived? Jésus didn't know. Too long ago. How could Bitsy have gotten into town for the fishing trip? Jésus didn't know. What did he think happened? Jésus didn't know. Something about the set of his jaw made me wonder if he didn't know or didn't want to talk about it.

I considered trying to slip into our *casita* unseen just to see how Bitsy might have done it, but I was here to ask questions. To get answers to those questions I would have to meet people, build some trust, develop relationships. Might as well start at the front desk.

The suite was in my name, so I did all the talking at the registration desk, showed my travel agent's IATA identification card, gave the hostess a business card. Sam hung back, still looking half asleep. He hardly seemed to be there at all. So much for the protection of traveling with a man, not to mention a police detective. I might as well have been alone.

Juanita was at the reception desk. Her English was accented but excellent. 'Ah, yes, Ms Hale, your *casita* is ready.' I had asked to be in the same suite that Bitsy had stayed in, and the resort was happy to comply. I filled out the usual papers. 'Just follow Manuel.' Manuel appeared, smiling, beside us.

Manuel led us back to the entrance where our luggage had been loaded on a golf cart decorated in the hotel's signature azure blue, yellow and orange. Manuel filled us in on the legend. A brilliant quetzalcoatl marked the front and all four sides of the canopy. The quetzalcoatl, the winged serpent bird, was the Aztec god of wind and wisdom. His worship in various Mexican cultures goes back to the first century BCE. Spanish conquistadores wrote about him, and some identified him with the explorer Cortes or Thomas the Apostle. I didn't know whether to hope we were protected by the wind or on our way to knowledge and wisdom. I could use a little wisdom.

Sam walked about two steps behind me, still silent. He had been perfectly alert on the plane, drinking nothing but orange juice and water. I tried to fight my annoyance by reminding myself that I was tired; I'm always tired when I travel, and when I'm tired I get grouchy and irritable. I tried to ignore him.

Sam and I sat behind Manuel as he drove us on winding paths toward the back of the resort. 'Here it is more private,' he said, smiling. The quiet hum of the electric cart's tires fit the resort's controlled perfection. Manicured grass and landscaping, no faded flowers. A housekeeper walking across the lawn stooped to pick up a fallen leaf. The sky was unbelievably blue, unnaturally blue except that it was undeniably natural. Flowers bloomed everywhere, and an exotic scent hung in the air. Staff, all neatly uniformed, smiled and nodded as we passed.

Manuel pointed out the locations of the spa facilities, the pools, tennis courts, the dining rooms, the beginnings of walking trails.

'You speak excellent English,' Sam said to Manuel.

'Thank you, *señor*. I attended college in the States. Arizona State, Hotel Management, and I'm working on an MBA.'

So much for my pitiful Spanish. 'Really?'

'Yes. Distance learning. Most of it's online, but our class meets on campus a couple of times each semester.'

Manuel stopped in front of a small building. Separated from several similar buildings by strategic landscaping and the layout of the paths, it gave an illusion of complete privacy. Manuel opened the door, and Sam and I walked into our own little world. A two-bedroom world. While Manuel went back for our bags, we looked around.

A frosty glass pitcher of sangria sat with two glasses on a table which commanded a view of the terrace outside our *casita*. Beyond the terrace, complete with brilliant flowers and chattering birds, were purple mountains and, in the far distance, a glimmer which had to be the sea. The sangria pitcher sat in a large bowl of ice, very little of which had

melted. It had to have been put here while we were on our
way from the lobby.

There was a quiet knock on the door. Manuel opened it to
admit a young woman and turned to us. 'Elena will unpack
your bags if you like.' He poured sangria into the two glasses.
'Is there anything else I can do for you?'

I looked at Sam, who looked as overwhelmed as I felt. I
had traveled a lot, but this level of pampering was rare. He
shrugged. 'I don't think so, Manuel. Thank you,' I said. 'There
is one thing, though.' I told him about Bitsy and why I had
come. 'You've been so attentive.' I motioned toward Elena,
already opening my luggage in one of the large bedrooms off
the sitting room where we had entered. 'How could my friend
not have been seen?'

'Many of our guests travel with their own staffs, Ms Hale.
Especially if one comes, what is the word, not wishing to
be seen or recognized, we would respect her wishes and leave
her alone. A driver might take such a one directly here, bring
in the luggage and leave immediately.'

I nodded, still not quite convinced. I certainly had had plenty
of attention already. 'Do you remember anything about her?'
I pulled the photo from my bag.

'Since you first called and the American police called, I've
heard of her, of course. Maria talked with all the staff, and
we have talked some between ourselves, but I am sorry. I do
not recognize her. This is the *casita* where she stayed,' he
added. 'Maria said you would prefer that.' He looked around
and shrugged. 'I'm sorry. I wish I could help you.' Manuel
waited. 'Is there anything else?'

'No, thank you,' I said.

Sam reached into his pocket and pulled out some folded
bills.

Manuel stopped him, backing away with his hands in
front of him. '*Gracias, señor*, but I cannot accept. Thank
you.' Manuel let himself out the front door, leaving Sam
and me taking in the opulence around us. Gratuities were
not accepted. More luxury.

At the center of the sitting room was a sunken area with
upholstered couches surrounding an open fire pit. A hood rose

above it to the vaulted ceiling above to carry smoke out of the room. A kitchen area was opposite the bedrooms, just beyond the table, with a hooded cooking island. Blue sky poured through windows in every direction. Soft, patterned rugs stretched across large terracotta tiles. I wanted to sink into one of the soft, pillowy sofas, put my feet up and go to sleep. Sam did. Or, at least, he stretched out and closed his eyes, but I reminded myself of why I had come.

'Elena.' She emerged from a bedroom as I called her name. 'May I ask you a few questions?' I asked. She smiled. I held Bitsy's photo out to her. She looked and nodded, still smiling. 'Do you remember seeing my friend here? She stayed in this *casita*.' Elena kept smiling but didn't say a word. 'Did you see her?' I tried to indicate *here* with my hands.

'*No habla Inglés.*' Still Elena smiled.

I tried to resurrect my high school Spanish and wished I hadn't spent so much time in that class flirting with Rick Jennings who only broke my heart anyway in the end. '*Mi amigo, amiga.* Did you *véase, ve*, see her? *Ici*?' No, that's French. '*Aquí*? Here?'

Elena kept smiling as she backed toward the door. 'No, *señorita*. No. *Buenos dias.*'

Sam opened his eyes as the door clicked shut. 'Not much so far. What's next, *señorita*?'

'I thought you were the hotshot detective, but all you've done is sleep.'

'In Nashville, I'm a hotshot detective. Out of my jurisdiction here. Here I'm a *gringo* tourist. And I must say I like it.' He raised one hand and snapped his fingers. I stared at him. 'I'm waiting for that sangria to materialize in my hand. I must not have it down yet.' He snapped a couple more times. 'I'll keep working on it. I figured if anyone was inclined to share some information, they'd be more likely to do it if they didn't think a policeman was hanging on every word.'

I don't know if he could actually see smoke rising from my ears or if something in my expression gave my feelings away. Sam put up his hands in surrender.

'OK. OK. Here's what we know so far. Nobody knows

anything. *Nada.* A rich American guest disappears, and there's this much attention, local police, State Department inquiries, private investigators, us, and everybody's friendly and polite, but that's all. Now, that's unusual. Most times, there'd be lots of talk among the staff, lots of people remembering things that didn't even happen maybe, just because they want to believe they're part of something big, something exciting, their fifteen minutes. Everybody remembers a conversation, a significant look, something they look back on and think was odd. Here? *Nada.* I don't think that happens by accident. Everybody we've met has been told – by someone who has some control over them, maybe their jobs, whatever – that they are to remember nothing. Maybe that's fairly innocent; the spa doesn't want bad press to scare away American tourists. Maybe there's something more going on. I don't know yet. I think a lot of people we meet are just not going to understand English. No matter that their jobs involve talking to Americans all day. *No habla Inglés.* Now, maybe the hotel's just afraid of legal liability or bad publicity, and they want to distance themselves from the whole thing. Could be. But there's an orchestrated response here. It's polite; it's friendly; but it's not supposed to tell us a thing.'

'So what do we do?'

Sam patted the couch. 'We relax. We tour. Maybe then somebody else will relax.' He closed his eyes again.

THIRTY-TWO

I gave up. I unpacked the rest of my things. I didn't bother waking Sam to ask which room he preferred. I decided I liked the one where Elena had already unpacked some of my luggage. White walls, desert colors in the bedcover and pillows. Tile floors in here, too, and rustic rugs woven with multicolored birds in rows. A king-sized bed faced a large window with a view of the mountains. I looked into the bath to see high windows, open to exotic smells from the garden, letting light into the large bath. I decided I'd just lie down for a minute, then take a shower and get to work. I stretched out on the bed and woke up nearly three hours later to find Sam sitting beside me holding a glass of sangria.

'You need to keep your fluids up in high desert, although this may not be the best way to do that. There's probably not much alcohol in this, though. Feel better?'

I'm not at my best when I first wake up. Especially in a strange room with a strange man (well, sometimes he's a little strange) sitting on the bed beside me. I was disoriented. I was fuzzy. And I was fairly sure I had drooled. I blinked, sat up and drank the sangria. 'Whoa!'

'Awake now?' he asked solicitously.

I rubbed my eyes and tried very hard to get all the way awake. I wanted to be coherent before I spoke. I nodded.

'What do you want to do about dinner?'

I looked at my watch. Seven thirty!

'I know it's Mexico,' he said, 'and nobody eats early here, but I'm kind of hungry.'

'Mnnhmm.' That was coherent, wasn't it?

'I'm not trying to rush you, but I thought you'd want to eat in the dining room. We could order room service, but I think we need to get out there, be seen.'

I nodded. 'Yeah, OK. I'll just take a quick shower.'

'No rush. I'll be out in the sitting room.' Too generous.

The shower worked. I blew my hair dry and twisted it up to save time. I pulled on a sundress covered with bright flowers, sandals, five minutes worth of makeup, and I was ready. I opened the door to find Sam outside in the living room dressed in khakis, a pink polo shirt and a linen jacket. He looked good. Real good. I don't know why I had expected the wrinkled dark suit he usually had on by the end of a long work day at home. This was a different look, and I liked it. A lot.

'Wow,' he said. 'You look great.'

That was exactly the right thing to say. Nothing about waiting, about being hungry, about my making fun of him, then sleeping the day away. 'Thanks.'

He opened the door, and we walked out into a perfect evening.

'I don't know how to find the dining room. I'll go back
inside and call,' I offered.

'I know,' he said confidently. 'This way.'

'How? You were asleep.'

'I wasn't asleep.'

'You sure looked like it.'

'That's why I'm the hotshot detective.'

THIRTY-THREE

D inner lived up to the resort's reputation. We were
seated outside on a terrace with a full moon so perfect
I suspected it might have been ordered for a photo
shoot. I had a mesquite-grilled swordfish so fresh it must have
been leaping in the blue water that morning.

'The fishing charter,' I remembered. 'We need to talk to
the fishing charter people.'

'Well, we need to think about that,' he said. 'I called the
concierge desk this afternoon. We can go tomorrow, if you
want. They have space. Or if you want to wander around some
tomorrow, we can go the next day. A driver will pick us up
at eight. We'll get back in about four.'

'All day, huh?'

'Yep.'

I nodded, resigned. 'OK.'

'Look. What questions are you planning to ask that you think
the police haven't already asked? And people doing business
here? They've got a lot more reason to talk to the local police
than they do to you. If we're going to learn anything, we're
going to learn it by not being police. We'll spend the day fishing,
being paying customers, and we'll talk. And listen.'

I nodded. He made sense. 'OK. What do you think, then,
tomorrow or Saturday?'

He thought. 'Saturday. That's what most people would do.
Take the first day easy. Have a massage. Lie by the pool.
Wander around town in the afternoon.'

'OK. You're the hotshot.'

He grinned over his grouper, and we left Bitsy and her grieving family for *mañana*. There was candlelight, good food, and I was having dinner with a handsome man. We sat and talked and laughed in perfect moonlight over perfect coffee brought by a perfect *mesero*. Our talk turned to ordinary things, where I'd traveled before, where he had. Vacations with his daughter. He laughed about a five-year-old Julie taking home shells and keeping them, unwashed, in a box under her bed until the smell demanded attention. I skirted mention of his ex-wife, but he mentioned her naturally when he told stories about Julie from the days when he was married. Finally, we just sat and smiled.

'You ready?'

'Sure.' The night air was cool, and I shivered as I rose. Sam took off his jacket and put it around my shoulders. Just for a moment, we stood there, his hands on my shoulders, our faces close. As close as they could be, that is, with Sam towering over me. We started back to the *casita*.

'You've done a good job,' I said. 'You're a good father, and it shows in Julie.'

He shrugged. 'She's a good kid. Her mother's been a big part of this, too.' I nodded. Refreshing not to hear a single father diss his ex-wife.

We walked on. Sam took my hand, and we followed the path toward the *casita*. At the door, Sam unlocked and opened the door, closed it behind us, and there, lit by moonlight spilling in through windows and skylights, he pulled me to him and kissed me. Long. I put my arms around his neck and kissed him back. Long. Then we were stumbling to the big couch, he was moving his hands through my hair, and we were still kissing.

He groaned. He crushed me to him. 'Campbell.'

'Mmm?' OK, not profound, but I'm not sure my primary blood flow was directed toward my brain.

'Campbell.' He sat up, pulled me to him again, then got up and walked to the kitchen.

What just happened here? Sam banged his head against the refrigerator then opened it.

'Want some water?' he asked. I shook my head. What was he doing? What was going on? He got out a bottle, opened it and took a long drink. 'I need to tell you something,' he said.

I waited. He wasn't married, so it couldn't be that.

Sam walked back into the living room and sat down beside me. 'I have a seventeen-year-old daughter.'

'Right.' I knew that. I really didn't want to hear anything strange or kinky.

'It's not easy raising a teenage girl these days. It's not easy *being* a teenage girl these days.'

No argument. I waited. He took another drink of water.

'I've had *the talk* with Julie. More than once really. And I'm sure her mother has, too.'

I nodded – encouragingly, I hoped.

'I've always tried to be honest with her. I've tried to talk straight. I've talked to her about sex and the diseases, of course, and getting pregnant, no means no, but more than that, I've tried to talk to her about relationships and values. Maybe I'm old-fashioned, but I see a lot of destructive behavior. Everybody talks about drugs and alcohol, but I see a lot of kids messed up because of sex, too. And it's useless to talk to kids about sex and love, because they're always in love.' He took a deep breath, looking straight ahead, not at me.

He had me worried when he brought up disease.

'Anyway,' he continued, 'I asked Julie not to have sex before she's married. No way I can be sure, of course, or enforce that. And a lot of people don't think that's realistic these days, but I think it is. I think it makes a lot of difference in a kid's focus in these years. But . . .'

I decided it was a safe bet those talks with Julie had been pretty uncomfortable for everyone.

'But she asked me, "What about you, Dad?" And she had a point. I was single. Was I asking her to do something that didn't apply to me? So we made a deal. She would wait until she got married, and so would I. I mean . . .'

Now he turned to look at me. He took my hand.

'What was I going to say? You know?'

I nodded.

'But I can't say I've always done what I thought was right. And it's not easy. Believe me, it's not easy right now. But I can remember seventeen. It's not easy then either, and that was the deal.'

I was doing a lot of nodding, but what was I supposed to say?

'And just when do you tell a woman this?' he asked. 'You don't meet somebody and say, "Oh, by the way, I won't sleep with you. Well, not unless we get married." Then when? First date? Third? I don't want to be making assumptions. So mostly I just avoid the situation. So. There it is. I like you. A lot. And I want to be straight with you.'

I nodded. 'Thanks.'

'You're a beautiful woman.'

I didn't know about that, but I'd forgive him that one lie.

'I like being with you. But I want to go back and be able to look Julie in the eye and tell her I haven't broken the deal. And she will ask. She will ask.' He stopped.

I nodded. 'I . . . I respect that. I appreciate your being honest with me. Really.' What else was I going to say? And, besides, I meant it. Of course, I meant it. I just wasn't sure how I was supposed to react, how I was supposed to feel. I didn't know how I did feel.

'We were having a great evening until I ruined it, weren't we?' he asked.

'It's still a beautiful evening.' Yeah, but it was over. That's the thing about honesty. No illusions.

Silence. Really uncomfortable silence.

'So,' I finally said. 'What do we do tomorrow, Hotshot?'

Sam laughed, relieved to change the subject. Suddenly he was all business, in control and in his comfort zone. 'Room service breakfast, I think. If Bitsy didn't go to the dining rooms, that must be what she did. And somebody had to bring it. Then you go to the spa, have a massage or something. Ask a few questions, not too much. I'll find a bar. Is there a bar in this place, or is that not healthy enough?'

'I'll bet you can find a celery juice on the rocks.'

'Does celery juice loosen tongues?' He didn't sound convinced.

'Tips might,' I suggested.

'I'll wander around, maybe go work out, maybe swim, see what I can find. Then, in the afternoon, we'll go into town. We've got a driver booked. We'll find out where guests go down in town, any restaurants the staff usually recommend, any particular shops. We take your photo of Bitsy, show it around some. It's a long shot. It's always been a long shot.'

'OK. Sounds like a plan.'

Sam sat there a moment then leaned over and kissed me again – but lightly this time. 'I guess I'll go to bed. Maybe take a shower.'

I nodded. 'OK.' I seemed to be saying that a lot, and I wasn't at all sure everything was OK. 'See you in the morning.'

He got up and started toward his room.

'Sam.' He turned. 'Uh . . . thank you. I mean it . . . I mean, I wasn't expecting . . . but. Anyway. Thank you for being honest.'

He nodded and went to his room.

I wasn't a slut. Really. I wasn't expecting to sleep with Sam on this trip. I really was here to find out what I could about Bitsy. And get out of Tennessee winter. I guess I just liked the idea of being able to say no. Assume. I remembered what my driver education teacher said that makes of 'u' and 'me'.

I got a bottle of water after all and went to my own room. The moonlight was still spilling in, but it wasn't quite the same with just me and my book.

THIRTY-FOUR

The next morning was bright and sunny. A new day.

I showered, dressed and opened my bedroom door to see Sam look up from breakfast. 'Hey, good morning. Want something to eat? I went ahead and ordered, but if you don't like it, we can call for something else.'

I looked over the table. I could call for something else if there was anything left in the kitchen. 'No. Thanks.' I sat

down. What else could there possibly be to order? Flowers.
Fruit. Croissants and muffins. A couple of omelets, eggs
Benedict. Juice, fresh squeezed. Coffee, regular and decaf.
Other odds and ends. I looked at him. Breakfast looked good,
and he looked good at the breakfast table, too. Dangerous
thoughts. Bitsy, I reminded myself. I was there to look for
Bitsy, not to fantasize about attractive and way too moral single
fathers.

'I didn't know what you'd want. You don't have to eat it
all.' He looked embarrassed.

'Good.' I'm not too chatty first thing in the morning
anyway, and this spread had me speechless.

'I looked at the last few weeks from Bitsy's day planner,'
Sam told me. 'They emailed scans from the lab.'

'What did you find?' I was awake now – and hopeful.

Sam grimaced. 'Nothing much. Some school stuff that you'd
expect. Nothing about a trip. All those appointments she missed
are in there. Your name's there for yesterday.'

'My name?'

'Yep. Were you expecting to see her?'

'No.'

Sam nodded. 'There was a question mark by your name.
Maybe she was planning to ask you to lunch or something.
Nothing else about travel. Do you know what "d n" might mean?'

DN. DN. 'No. Why?'

'Those letters are in there two days before she disappeared.
Lower case. Initials?'

We were both silent. Thinking. I couldn't come up with
anything 'd n' might mean. I poured myself some coffee and
started to eat.

'Good, huh?' Sam asked.

'Yeah. Great. It's going to be tough to go back to grapefruit
juice in the car on the way to work.'

'Jésus brought it.'

'Jésus from yesterday?'

He nodded. 'Still friendly, still knows nothing about Bitsy.
I think we're bonding.'

'Really?'

'Yep. We talked fishing. Man talk. You wouldn't understand.'

He grinned and moved the coffee pots just far enough that I couldn't easily reach them to throw at him.

I ignored the dig. 'Does Jésus fish a lot?'

'He does. He and his brothers have a boat. They make a good little second income from it. He says the fishing charter is a good one. Good value, boats maintained well, pretty much honest, he says, and the guides know the water, know the weather and fishing patterns. His uncle works on the dock there.'

'Big family,' I offered. 'Did you learn anything else, anything other than fishing tips?'

He looked at me sadly, mock offense in his expression. 'You think I'm not taking this seriously. If I'd just ordered coffee and toast, Jésus and I wouldn't have had as much time to talk.' He ate a bite of the muffin he had just buttered. 'But the answer to your question is not yet. Not yet. But I'm working on it. You, on the other hand' – he pointed his butter knife – 'are sleeping on it.'

Touché. 'Yeah, well. I'm just an amateur. You're the professional.'

He smiled. Graciously. Patronizingly. Infuriatingly. But it was hard to stay annoyed at a man who had eggs Benedict and fresh orange juice waiting for me when I woke up. I trusted that my silence while I ate was punishment enough.

THIRTY-FIVE

As I lay on the massage table with my stress melting, I decided I owed it to my commitment to professionalism to do this kind of thing more often. I believed I could go home and sell this pretty effectively. It was wonderful. Deep tissue massage. Soothing music. Aromatherapy. I relaxed and breathed deeply. I could easily see Bitsy running to a place like this to escape. And it reminded me why I love my job. Now that I was here, being pampered before I could even imagine what I wanted, running away from home seemed like a good idea.

'*Señorita* Hale?' A quiet voice interrupted. '*Señorita* Hale? Some papaya juice, *patita*? *Por favor.* Drink juice. Fluid is *muy*, ah, important.'

There you go. Papaya juice. I love papaya juice. I hadn't thought about it, but yeah, I was thirsty. I sat up, drank my *patita* and lay back for my reflexology massage. And talked.

'I came here because my friend said it was the most wonderful place she'd ever been. She was right. Bitsy Carter. She was here about a month ago. Did you happen to meet her?'

'*Señorita* Carter? Ahh . . .'

'*Señora* Carter. She is blonde, a little taller than me? A little thinner than me.'

'I cannot say. *Lo siento*, sorry. Is this too hard?'

'No. It feels great. *Gracias.*'

'*Sí. De nada.*'

She continued massaging my foot, putting pressure on one area after another, explaining what part of my body or function would be affected by that area. I didn't care. It just felt good.

I brought the conversation back to Bitsy.

'She was even in the same *casita* that I'm in.' I told her which *casita* Sam and I were staying in. No luck.

'*Lo siento, señorita. No recuerdo. No* . . . remember? I will give you this chart to take home. You can continue this when you are home. This' – she dug in with emphasis, and it was the most delicious pain – 'will help your lower back.' She touched a spot in my back that always hurt when I sat too long, especially after a long flight or drive. 'Especially here.'

I believed. I believed. I promised myself to massage my feet every night. But I was pretty sure it wouldn't feel as good as this.

Two hours later, after a mud mask and wrap, through which I napped with cucumber slices on my eyes, I had no new information, but I was refreshed and ready to take on the world. I sipped one more glass of juice and headed back to the *casita* to find Sam.

He was just out of the shower, dressed in khaki shorts and

a light blue polo, drops of water still in his hair, which stood up in spikes like a twelve year old's.

He looked at me. 'You look mellow. More relaxed than I've ever seen you, I think, except when you were in the hospital and drugged.' Sam had been there one night, part of the night anyway, after my poking around put me and my Spider up close and personal with a tree, leaving me hospitalized with a concussion. It was a long story.

'I feel wonderful. You'll get no argument from me today.'

Sam looked skeptical. 'We'll see.'

Sam handed me a message from the manager, Maria, that he had found when he returned to the *casita*. She had pulled records from the time of Bitsy's stay. After Bitsy checked in, there was no other record of her stay. No room service orders, no spa treatment schedules, no phone calls or other incidental charges. No concierge requests. No record that anyone here had booked her fishing trip. Nothing. She had paid in advance, checked in, gone fishing and disappeared.

I dressed quickly, and we walked to the reception area.

Jésus was waiting to take us into town. '*Buenos dias, señorita*. You look *muy bonita* this afternoon.'

'*Gracias*, Jésus. Where should we have lunch today?'

'In the town, *señorita*?'

'*Sí.*'

'What would you like to have?'

'Good, authentic Mexican food that's safe for our delicate *gringo* stomachs. Where do you suggest?'

'Ah, *sí*, such a strong country, such weak stomachs.' He smiled. 'My favorite is Caliente. Is good food. My cousin is the cook. I will tell him to make his specialty for you.'

'What is his specialty?'

Jésus shrugged. 'Today I don't know, but it will be good.'

'Your cousin's restaurant. Is that where you usually take guests from the spa?' Sam asked.

Jésus shook his head. 'Many guests go to Ixtapa. *Muy* . . . how do you say . . . lights, shine? Very nice, but not the real Zihuatanejo.'

Ixtapa was a resort town four miles away, its location picked by a computer. The Mexican government had developed it in the seventies. High-rise hotels, everything relatively new. We probably should have gone there, too, to ask around, but it was much more a tourist center. Sam and I had thought there was a better chance that Bitsy would be remembered in the smaller fishing village. And we knew she had come here. She'd caught that huge marlin here.

Jésus continued, 'Many guests want American food. They come to Zihuatanejo and want a hamburger. They want McDonald's; then they say is not like McDonald's at home.' He shrugged again. 'Why do they come?'

Sam nodded. 'The American lady we're looking for, *Señora* Carter, I don't think she would have been looking for a hamburger. When you or one of the other drivers take guests into town, where do you usually suggest they go?'

Jésus thought. 'If not Caliente, maybe Casa Fiesta. To shop, maybe La Señorita or Plata for jewelry. Maybe A La Deriva for souvenirs, crafts. There are small shops near the docks; people usually go there. I myself would recommend La Mina. My sister works there.' He smiled. A really big family.

'Thanks,' Sam said. 'That will give us a start.'

Jésus smiled and nodded. 'I tell you,' he said suddenly, 'I help. I ask about the lady. You give me picture, and I talk to my sister, my cousin. They will ask. A person may talk to me or to them and not' – he looked apologetic – 'to *gringos*. I will help you.'

'We'd appreciate that,' Sam said.

We spent the rest of the drive curving down from the mountains to the sea, looking at the incredible view of the approaching ocean, too blue to be believed, and planning where to go. That is, listening to Jésus plan. Jésus' plan for Sam and me seemed to involve spending money at places owned by Jésus' relatives while he asked the questions.

Our first stop was Zihuatanejo Fishing Charters. It was a small, wooden building, not much more than a shack, at the docks. Fishing boats bobbed in the water, jostling against each other like a bunch of children anxious for a teacher's attention.

The building itself had been painted white but not recently.

The trim had been bright, and it seemed to have been done whenever the whim took the painter and he had leftover paint from a boat. The door and facing were a bright marine blue. One window had once been red; a few sheltered spots testified to that. Now it was mostly a weathered pink. Another window was yellow. Faded green and a lighter shade of blue were in other spots. Maybe it was just that the colors of the sea and sky and sun were so brilliant everything manmade faded in comparison.

A chalkboard by the front door listed record catches in various species of fish as well as the top catches for the past week. If I'd known more about deep-sea fishing, I might have been more impressed. I did notice that Bitsy's huge marlin was nowhere near the record. Flag poles mounted beside the door held Mexican and US flags as well as a port banner and a company banner. Matching banners flew from four or five boats tied up nearby.

To the right of the door, below the flag poles, was a board listing ships and their captains. The *Dorado Queen* was on the list, third from the top. The *Dorado Queen* with her captain Mick Mikwozhewski was at sea that afternoon, carrying the Timo party from Japan, and wasn't due in for several hours. But the *Dorado Queen* wasn't listed on tomorrow's list. I was hoping that meant that tomorrow she and Captain Mick were available.

Inside, I recognized Sally O'Hara from the photo on the website. She was one of the owners of Zihuatanejo Fishing Charters, a woman who had spent too much time in the sun, forty-ish, with brown hair sun-bleached in streaks and wrinkles etched around her eyes from laughing in the sun.

She looked up from a ledger propped on the counter. 'Hello. I'm gonna guess that you speak better English than Spanish. How can I help you?' Boston? Providence? It was definitely a New England accent. She wore a faded blue T-shirt and tan shorts.

Sam spoke. 'We'd like to go out tomorrow.'

'Sure. Looks like the weather's going to be great. And the fishing sure has been. Let's see.' She pulled out a list and ran her finger down it. 'Tomorrow . . . Look's like we've got the

Dorado Queen and *Marlin's Blues*. Both are good ships, captains who know the waters.'

I looked at Sam. He pretended to hesitate, looked at me. I shrugged. 'You decide.'

'The *Dorado Queen*,' he said decisively.

'Good choice. You'll like Captain Mick. Fish practically jump in his boat.' She grinned. 'I'm co-owner, bookkeeper, cheerleader here.' She pulled a form from beneath the counter. 'Where ya' from?'

'Nashville,' I said.

'Tennessee! Home of the Grand Ole Opry. We had Toby Keith down here last month. Caught some big fish. You guys country music fans?'

'Of course. It's hard not to be in Nashville,' I answered.

Sally nodded, pushing the form across the counter between Sam and me. 'I just need you to fill this out, sign down here. We supply the gear and tackle, your lunch, drinks, ice. We need a fifty-dollar deposit. You can pay the rest in the morning.'

The form had spaces for our names, addresses, passport numbers, phone numbers at home and local contact information. Above the space for our signatures was a waiver indemnifying Zihuatanejo Fishing Charters in case we didn't return in one piece. Sam gave his credit card for the deposit.

Sally asked what we wanted for lunch, whether we wanted beer or soft drinks and juice, checked off some boxes and looked up. 'You're all set. We'll see you in the morning. You're up at the spa? Just let the concierge desk know and they'll have a driver ready to get you down here on time. I don't think there'll be anybody else on your boat, though. Any questions?'

Sam and I couldn't think of any questions about fishing, and we were saving the ones we were itching to ask for tomorrow.

'OK, then, we'll see you in the morning. Bring a hat and something with sleeves, sunscreen. See you then.'

We spent the rest of the afternoon with Jésus, having excellent fajitas at his cousin's restaurant, poking around in little shops, watching as he showed Bitsy's picture and urged his friends and cousins to remember something. *Nada*. Headshakes, shrugs. We headed back up the mountain in the fading light with nothing to show for our time but a few souvenirs and, for me, gifts for family and friends back home: a shawl, a set of linen napkins with a quetzalcoatl embroidered on each and two really lovely silver hair clasps: one for me and one for Sam's daughter Julie.

THIRTY-SIX

That night I had time to do it right when I got ready for dinner. My hair was right, thanks to the low humidity of the high desert. I had time to do my makeup right, and I'd gotten just enough sun that afternoon to add a little color without burning. I wore my favorite dress, a blue silk sheath that made me look better than anything else I own. I'm always grateful for a good optical illusion. I saw Sam's eyes widen when I came into the sitting room. That was the effect I was going for. I was intensely aware of his hand, warm on my back, as we walked through the flower-scented twilight to the dining room.

Dinner, again, was off duty, except that we kept our ears open. No talk of Bitsy. No reminders of Thompson and Rachel. We laughed, tasted each other's entrees, joked with the waiter.

'You gonna cook this when we get home?' Sam asked after I had asked the waiter how the shrimp sauce was made.

'You're calling me out, aren't you? You catch it, I'll cook it.'

Sam looked years younger than he did in Nashville. It was partly the sun, I guessed. A little sun made everyone look better, softer, more relaxed.

'When was the last time you had a real vacation?' I asked.

He shrugged, surprised by the question. 'I try to take Julie to the beach for a few days every year.'

I nodded.

'It's not the same, though, I guess. I mean, when you go somewhere with your kid, especially when they're teenagers, you're so conscious of being glad they'll still go with you, of the time slipping away. You want to do things they want to do. And you want to make sure they're safe. You relax, but not in the same way.' He shrugged again. 'And I always seem to be in the middle of a case.'

I understood. Even when I traveled, I was on duty. Always evaluating, making notes, mental and otherwise, for clients. Would I recommend the destination? Which hotels, which restaurants? What would you wish you had known before you came? Wandering through Kensington Gardens was better than sitting in the office, but there was always an element of work. I picked through my fruit, fresh tropical fruit outside on a patio with cool tropical mountain air warmed by chimineas, and thought, what the heck am I whining about?

After dinner, we took the long way back, lingering to look at the lights from Zihuatanejo and Ixtapa below, at the stars and moon above. 'Here,' Sam said. 'Wear my coat. You'll freeze.' He was right. The shawl I'd bought from Jésus' mother's second cousin was not enough for the chilly night. I took his coat without guilt. He did have on long sleeves. Shallow as always, I'd opted to look good.

'Thanks.' When he helped me shrug into his coat, his hands stayed on my shoulders. I leaned against him. For warmth. Yeah, sure. But he wrapped his arms around me, and he was warm and he felt so good.

When we got back to the *casita*, the sitting room was washed with moonlight pouring through the skylight. Neither of us turned on a light.

'You want a fire?' Sam asked.

'Sure. Want something to drink?' I asked, but I didn't care. I didn't want anything to drink myself; I just wanted an excuse to keep this from ending.

'I guess,' Sam said. 'Maybe something hot, tea, coffee.'

Sam found matches and lit the gas logs. I put on water to boil for tea.

'Need some help?' Sam asked.

'No, thanks. What do you drink in your tea? Milk, sugar,

honey, lemon?' Suddenly I realized that I was nervous. More nervous than last night.

'Lemon, sugar.' He sat on the sofa.

I fixed the tea and brought it to the table in front of him.

We drank our tea without saying much of anything. Then in front of the fire and under the Mexican moon, we necked like teenagers until we fell asleep there on the sofa.

THIRTY-SEVEN

I woke the next morning to a knock on the door. I blinked and looked around.

Sam was coming out of his room, already showered and dressed, a towel in his hand and his hair damp. 'I'll get it. We've got almost an hour before we need to leave.'

I nodded. Sam had put a throw over me some time last night or this morning. He was fresh from the shower, and I was wearing last night's clothes. I bet my mascara was smeared, too. I headed to my room and closed the door as he opened the front door to Jésus and breakfast. I heard the murmur of their talking as I took my clothes off and started the shower. Thirty minutes later, I was clean, myself, and ready for breakfast. Sam was reading an English language newspaper.

'I had Jésus bring you back some fresh coffee. It's good and hot.'

'Thanks.'

'You know, there seems to be a pretty large expatriate American community here. Big enough, at least, to support a local English paper. It has some stuff from the US, national politics, the Mexican president's been to Washington, a blizzard in the upper Midwest.' A little gloating there. I nodded, my mouth full, while I buttered a croissant. Sam went on. 'There's a business section with stuff about American businesses operating in the area, some social stuff. Even a sort of gossip column, "Coconut Telegraph". Might be some sources there.' He looked up. 'The thing is, if there are that many Americans, particularly a tight little community of people who see themselves as . . . outlaws, exiles, expatriates, adventurers, then you could probably find somebody who'd do most anything you'd want. That is, if somebody wanted something done to Bitsy while she was here.'

'Somebody?'

Now it was Sam's turn to nod. 'I think I'll stick this in my bag, so the maid won't throw it away when she cleans.'

I finished breakfast, and we both gathered up what we needed for the day. Hats – Sam's was a faded triple-A Nashville Sounds hat – sunscreen, long-sleeved shirts in case we needed a layer over our T-shirts and shorts. I put Bitsy's photographs, business cards, some cash, my passport and credit cards in a small nylon shoulder backpack and left my purse in a drawer underneath my clean underwear.

We walked out our front door and Jésus drove up in a golf cart. 'We ready?' he asked.

'We ready,' Sam confirmed.

THIRTY-EIGHT

Jésus zipped us around the grounds to the entrance and, once we were in the jeep, down the mountain to Zihuatanejo. He kept up a constant chatter, swerving around curves without seeming to look, one hand off the wheel as he gestured, then the other. I tried not to think about it. By the time we slowed down for traffic in Zihuatanejo, I was looking forward to the calming contrast of tossing around in a small boat for a while.

Sally O'Hara was loading drinks and food onto the *Dorado Queen* when we slid into her parking lot. 'Hello!' she shouted. 'Come on in. Let's get the paperwork out of the way so you guys can get on the water and catch some fish.' We followed her inside, and she opened a folder on the counter. 'Here we go. Have you done this before?'

Sam nodded. I said no.

'Oh, well, you're gonna have a great time. The weather's perfect; blue water's close in; the fish are biting. And Captain Mick's a lot of fun.'

She told us what to sign and where. We paid. Then I pulled out the picture of Bitsy. 'We're here partly to look for a friend. She was here a few weeks ago.' I gave the date. 'Bitsy Carter.'

'Bitsy Carter.' The light bulb went on. 'Oh, yeah, caught a huge marlin. Not a record, but close. Huge. Said she'd never caught anything before. You're looking for her?'

'She didn't come home. Your blog is the last trace we have of her. We thought you might remember something she'd said, what her plans were. Well, not you, necessarily, but the captain. Maybe you could put us in touch with some people on the boat with her.'

'Sure. I'll do what I can. I wasn't out with her, so I didn't talk to her much, but I'll pull her file while you're out. I can't give you addresses for the people who were with her, but I can contact them, ask them to get in touch with you. Grab me when you come in.'

'Thanks.' I stuck the photos back in my bag. I had thought I might need to show them to Sally to jog her memory, but apparently Bitsy's fish was big enough to be memorable.

Outside, we met Captain Mick and Sally's partner, Tom Cooper. We shook hands all around as Tom and Captain Mick finished loading gear and food onto the boat. Tom and Sally wished us luck and moved on to ready another boat.

'All right, you guys ready to catch some fish?' Captain Mick asked if we all had sunscreen and offered us small tubes, just in case. I hadn't been asked if I had sunscreen this many times since the last time I'd been to the beach with my mother.

We assured him that we were ready for the fish and the sun and climbed on board. He gave us life vests and made sure we put them on correctly. 'Never needed 'em, never plan to. First day we don't use 'em, that's when something'll happen.' He told us where to sit while he got us out to the blue water, and we settled back.

It was a gorgeous day. Sailing is more my style, but it felt great skimming over the magically blue water, salt spray cooling the air, bouncing over small waves and heading out to sea. When I looked back, the mountains rose above the shrinking village and the beaches. Before we were out very far, we could see the high-rise hotels and condominiums of Ixtapa in the distance up the shore. There was too much noise to talk, but I looked at Sam and saw him smiling, too.

Captain Mick slowed the *Dorado Queen* and brought her to a gentle stop. He brought out cold drinks and started getting out the gear, setting up the reels, helping us put on the harnesses that supported the huge reels, finally baiting the lines with fish big enough to serve at dinner. Sam helped, but I just stayed out of the way. I'd fished in Percy Priest Lake back home in Nashville, and I could put a worm on a hook, but this tackle was something else.

THIRTY-NINE

C aptain Mick got everything set for us and went through his spiel: safety first; help each other out; drink lots of fluids; reapply the sunscreen; and, hey, we're here to have fun. Let's have some fun. Then I brought out the photographs.

Sally O'Hara had not been evasive. She hadn't told us anything yet, but her eyes hadn't shifted. Captain Mick Mikwozhewski's eyes shifted.

'Really? She was on my boat?' he asked, seeming to think it over. He shook his head. 'Doesn't ring any bells.'

'She caught a marlin, a five-hundred-sixty-eight-pound Pacific blue marlin.'

Captain Mick grinned, but his grin had lost a little of its nonchalance. We didn't seem to be having as much fun as a few minutes before. 'People generally do catch big fish on my boat. No brag, just fact. I can't remember 'em all.'

I forced myself not to look at Sam. Bitsy's marlin had certainly been memorable to Sally O'Hara.

Sam spoke first. 'Well, if you remember anything. You have a card, Campbell?'

I pulled a card out of my pouch and handed it to Captain Mick, wondering why I was wasting that much of some poor tree. Captain Mick would not be calling or emailing, I was sure. He nodded and stuck it in the pocket of his shirt.

Then Sam spoke again. 'Oh, hey, I have one of mine, after all. Hang on to it, too.' He shrugged. 'Just in case anything comes to you.'

I watched Captain Mick's face change as he read Sam's card. The gentle swells weren't bothering me, but I could have sworn that Captain Mick was looking a little queasy. 'You're a long way from your jurisdiction, aren't you?' he asked Sam.

Sam nodded. 'Yeah. I'm here for the fishing. Just asking a few questions, keeping an eye out for a friend of a friend.' He inclined his head toward me, his eyes never leaving Captain Mick's.

Captain Mick nodded, and I realized some alpha male thing had just happened. Challenges hung palpably in the air.

'So,' Sam continued, 'what should we be looking for out here?'

We fished.

I wasn't trying too hard. I watched the horizon rise and fall, drank my water and admired Sam's muscles when he would reel and wait, reel and wait. By the time we broke for lunch, we had a couple of decent swordfish on ice and had caught and released a small marlin. Lunch was simple but good, and we were hungry after the morning on the water: thick ham sandwiches on fresh, homemade bread with cheese and fruit. Captain Mick seemed at ease again, entertaining us with stories of the sea, dolphins more intelligent than his passengers, sharks he had faced. We caught and released a couple of tarpon and decided we were ready to head in.

Sam and I helped Captain Mick pack up the tackle and gear. He went into the tiny cabin and started up the engines. The quiet and peace of the sea was gone.

Captain Mick yelled back to us. 'Dolphins! Look!' He pointed behind the boat. 'Off to starboard there!'

I stood at the rail, watching the dolphins jumping and arcing in the distance. 'They're playing,' I yelled to Sam over the noise of the engines. He smiled. 'They have to be playing.'

Just then the idling engines roared, and the boat jumped, turning sharply to the port and bouncing over the waves. I felt myself flying over the rail and reached, grabbing for anything I could touch, but I felt only air and spray. I heard – or felt – cloth rip as Sam grabbed for me, catching first my shirt, then my leg. I slammed hard against the side of the boat, trying to stay away from the stern and the engines. Sam hung on as I scrabbled for something to hold onto. Salt spray filled my mouth and nose. I was coughing, choking.

I tried to grab a cleat, but I couldn't. Sam held on, pulling me back. I bounced as the boat did, slamming hard against the hull. I twisted, got an arm over the side. Sam pulled, and I pulled, and I slid over the side to collapse onto rope and gear.

Sam was yelling over the noise. 'Are you OK?'

The engines stopped abruptly, and Captain Mick took his time stepping over a cooler to reach us. 'Sorry.'

Maybe it had been seconds, minutes, but it had felt like forever. I remembered something my brother used to say: my life flashed before my eyes, and it was a short story. I don't like short stories. I prefer nice, long novels.

Sam ignored him. 'You OK?'

I nodded. OK? I guess. I was shaking, and a couple of scrapes were bleeding. I'd probably have some colorful bruises in the morning from where I'd crashed against the rail as Sam dragged me back, but I was OK. I thought. I held onto Sam.

Sam and Captain Mick locked eyes over my head.

'Sorry,' Captain Mick repeated. 'It's dangerous out here. That's why we insist on the life vests.' He unfastened a first-aid kit from the side of the boat and handed it to Sam. 'There're some antiseptic wipes in there. You don't want to risk infection. This isn't Disneyland. Anything could have happened to your friend, I guess.' Testosterone hung in the air again. 'You be careful.'

FORTY

The rest of the return trip was calm, but I stayed in my seat. Sam didn't say anything, but his jaw never unclenched. You don't want to start a fight with the only man who knows the way back to land. I could appreciate that.

Sally O'Hara came out of the office to meet us as we approached and helped tie up the boat. Her eyes took in my torn shirt and the bruises beginning to show on my legs. 'Everything OK?'

Captain Mick answered quickly. 'Sure. Little mishap when Miss Hale was watching dolphins.'

Sam and I were silent as Sally helped us out.

Sally looked sharply at him, and her face didn't relax as she helped Sam and me off the boat. 'Lunch OK?'

'Great,' I answered a little grimly. 'Really good.'

'I have some information for you,' she said. 'Not much, but I hope it helps. Come on in.'

I looked back as I followed her to see Sam and Captain Mick staring at each other again. Captain Mick smiled, not a friendly smile, more of a challenge. 'I'll load the cooler with your fish when the car from the spa gets here.'

Sam nodded almost imperceptibly before he turned to put his arm around me and followed Sally.

Inside, Sally opened a folder on the counter. 'Here's the information we have on your friend. I have here that a call came from the spa to book her trip, but nothing that says who called. Usually I put the name of the specific employee who calls. We like to thank them, send a little gift at Christmas to the local people who refer us. I don't know why that's not here. It was paid in advance by a credit card. Usually we'd require a signature and card imprint, but not necessarily if someone's staying at the spa.'

'What do you remember about her?' Sam asked.

Sally looked apologetic. 'Not much. It was a busy day. All the boats were full. We were trying to get a lot of people aboard.'

Sam and I looked over the form.

'You can keep this,' Sally said. 'It's a copy I made for you.' There was nothing on there we didn't know. Bitsy's home address, phone number, passport number, Tennessee driver's license number. Philip's name as next of kin. The address and phone number of the spa. Bitsy's credit card number, familiar by now. 'I had a copy of this photo printed out. We always take a photo of a big catch and send it to the guests.' She pushed the photo across to us, and I picked it up. It was a huge fish. The blonde woman beside it wasn't looking into the camera. She was turned toward the fish, her hair blowing in the wind to hide most of her face.

'This isn't Bitsy,' I said. 'Could you check again? I'm sorry you went to this trouble for the wrong picture, but this is someone else. Not Bitsy Carter.'

Sam took the photo. I pulled out the two I had brought.

Sally O'Hara looked confused. 'No, this is her,' she insisted. 'I remember. We don't see many fish that size. The print was in her file. I had saved it on the computer. This is a new print, but it matches the one in the file.' She looked at the close-up photo of Bitsy that I held. She frowned and held both photographs closer. 'They kind of look alike' – she shook her head – 'but this isn't the Bitsy Carter who fished with us.'

I pushed the other picture, wrinkled from a day fishing, across the counter to Sally. It was the one I'd found in my car when I left the Thompsons' house, the one that I didn't know who had put there. 'What about him?' I pointed to Philip. 'Ever seen him before?' I looked up at Sam as Sally O'Hara nodded.

'Maybe. I'm not sure, I think . . .' She tapped the photo of Philip Carter with her finger, then shrugged. 'He might have been here. I don't know. I couldn't tell you when.'

Sally promised to contact the other guests who had fished with the woman who had said she was Bitsy Carter and ask them to contact us. That didn't seem to have as much potential for helpful information as we had hoped. Sally checked her records, both computer and hard files, but found no record of a Philip Carter. We left photos with her, Philip's photo and the one I had brought of Bitsy, and she said she'd ask her partner Tom and all the captains what they could remember about either of them.

When we went outside, the *Dorado Queen* was empty but secured, and Captain Mick Mikwozhewski was nowhere to be seen. Jésus, though, was standing beside the spa shuttle and smiling.

'Good fishing. *Buena.* You will have for *cenar*, for dinner?'

'Will the chef cook one for us?' Sam asked.

'*Sí, sí*, of course. It will be *delicioso*,' Jésus assured us.

The drive up the mountain was quieter than the morning trip. We had plenty to think about, and I didn't know about Sam, but I was tired. Really tired. And starting to get sore. I rubbed my arm. Sam looked over and took my hand. He was still holding it when we pulled up to the spa entrance.

At the spa, Jésus assured us he would take our swordfish to the kitchen.

'The second one's for you,' Sam told him.

'*Gracias, Señor* Sam. The chef will cook it for all the staff. *Gracias.*'

'Let's walk,' Sam said, and we started up the path toward the *casita*. 'You don't want to get stiff.'

Right. I wanted a hot bath and a long nap. And some aspirin. And my own bed. And I was already stiff.

Sam unlocked the door of our *casita*, and we went inside. He closed the door behind us and put his arms around me. 'I'm sorry,' he said into my hair. 'I'm sorry. *Are* you OK?'

'Yeah, I'm fine. Really.'

'Nobody's going to remember anything about Philip.'

'No,' I agreed.

'But we certainly stirred something up here.'

We agreed on a time for dinner, and I went to my room. I took a long shower and collapsed on the bed. I woke up an hour later. A bottle of water and some aspirin were on the table beside the bed. What a man. I took the aspirin and drank the whole bottle of water. I felt better. I did my hair and got dressed. I didn't think the blue spots growing on my

skin brought out the color of my eyes, but I was hungry. I
draped a shawl over my shoulders to hide some of the bruises
and went out into the sitting room to find Sam waiting on
the sofa.

'I've seen you look worse,' he said, grinning.

'Thanks. I needed that.' What I really needed was an ice
pack.

'We need to go home.'

'I know.'

'It's not that I don't want to be here with you. It's not that.
But we've learned all we can here. The story's in Nashville.
Some important things happened here, but I don't think we're
going to be able to prove anything helpful here. I don't think
Bitsy was ever here.'

I nodded. 'I'll see about our reservations.' I called the airline
and moved our return reservations up. I called the concierge
desk and asked for a ride to the airport early the next morning.
'We can leave at eight tomorrow morning,' I told Sam.

He nodded, stood and held out his hand. 'Let's go eat some
swordfish.'

Dinner was *delicioso* again. Was the fish better because Sam
had caught it? I don't know, but it was good. Everything was
good. And apparently the one in the staff kitchen was good,
too. Waiters kept stopping by and thanking us. '*Gracias, señor,
señorita. Pez espada. Maravilloso.*' Marvelous swordfish.

We walked back holding hands. Inside the *casita*, standing
by the door, Sam kissed me. 'I guess I'd better pack,' he said,
brushing my hair back with his hand.

'Yeah,' I agreed.

'It's late.'

'Yep. We have to leave early.' And why start something
we're not going to finish?

'Yeah,' Sam agreed.

'It's been a long day.'

He nodded.

An hour or so later we went to pack.

FORTY-ONE

The flight home seemed to take forever. I kept trying to make sense of the pieces we had. Someone claiming to be Bitsy had been in Zihuatanejo. Had someone killed Bitsy, taken her identification and had a vacation with her identity and credit cards? If so, she hadn't spent as much as she could have. A frugal murderer-thief? And where was Bitsy? Had she made it to Mexico? Had someone followed her, targeted her when she got off the plane? Was Philip behind all this after all? Could Maureen be involved? Mark had hinted that Bitsy had a lover. Who? And where did he fit into this? And what exactly had Captain Mick Mikwozhewski been trying to hide?

'Move,' Sam said.

'What?' I wasn't taking more than my half of the armrest.

'Move. You need to move around. I've been in a few fights, come out of one or two looking worse than you do. Move around.'

I squirmed and stretched in my seat. I unbuckled and went to the restroom just for the fifteen-foot walk. When I got back to my seat, I tried to move each joint, and some were already complaining. But that was nothing to the way they screamed when I stood up and got off the plane in Houston. Thank goodness Sam grabbed my carry-on bag from the overhead compartment. I was grateful for the wide leather chairs in the executive lounge.

'Want something to drink?' Sam asked.

'Yes, thanks. Coke or water. Either.' I went to the restroom and inspected my bruises. They were really colorful now, blue, purple, a bit of red. Tinges of green emerging. A bit like a Paul Jenkins painting, only darker. And painful. I decided to avoid seeing my parents until the worst of it faded.

When I returned to our seats, Sam had brought me a Perrier and was already checking his email on his laptop. I took another couple of aspirin with the Perrier. I needed that – and a nap in something more comfortable than an airline seat or even a seat in a passenger lounge. I decided to call and check my phone messages. Most were routine. A reminder that I was to take meat loaf to church for Room in the Inn next week, a couple of telemarketing calls, then something that got my attention.

'Miss Hale,' a soft, feminine Irish whisper, 'don't call me back. Don't come to see me. I'll call you when I can.' Click.

I frowned. 'Sam,' I started, but he was looking at me, and I knew something was wrong. 'What? What is it?'

'Maureen Kennedy's dead. Broken neck. Fell off a horse at the Thompsons' farm.'

Sam pulled up the *Tennessean* website and found the story.

FORTY-TWO

Maureen had taken the children to the Thompsons' farm in Maury County, south of Nashville, to ride. Mr Thompson was a steeplechase jockey, an amateur sportsman in the classical sense, and the family had a stable full of their own horses as well as a few they boarded and trained. A resident farm manager had helped Maureen and the children saddle and mount the horses. Mr Thompson had been there at the time but had left the horse barn to go to the house after Maureen and the children rode off toward a 250-acre wooded area on the property. Rachel and Thompson had ridden back about forty-five minutes later to say that Maureen had fallen, and they couldn't wake her up. When the farm manager, a Rod Wagner, arrived, Maureen was dead. The Maury County coroner said her neck was broken. Philip Carter, Miss Kennedy's employer, had been shocked. 'My children have been through so much,' he was quoted as saying. 'Maureen's been such a rock to them since their mother's disappearance. We're all just in shock. And our hearts go out to Maureen's family.'

Funeral arrangements were incomplete pending the arrival of Miss Kennedy's family from Doolin, Ireland.

Sam emailed his office, directing the staff to request copies of the coroner's report and the Maury County sheriff's report on the accident.

A detective from Sam's office was waiting just past the security checkpoint when we landed in Nashville. His notebook was open, and he was filling Sam in on Bitsy's case and others as we walked to the baggage claim area. I hurried to keep up. They had found some good prints on the day planner, a Vietnam vet whose name matched the first name the homeless man had given the minister. They had a twenty-five-year-old military photo that the minister said could have been the man. The photo was being circulated among patrolmen, the Union Mission, downtown liquor stores, church homeless ministers. If he was still in Nashville, they'd find him, but they didn't know how much more help he'd be. The detective didn't sound optimistic.

Sam kept asking questions of Frank, the junior detective, as we waited for our bags. If I'd wondered how it would be once we got home, if the parting would be awkward, romantic, uncertain, I needn't have bothered. I was pretty much forgotten.

After we pulled the bags off the carousel, Sam turned to me. 'Look, I need to get to the office. Do you mind if Frank takes you home?' Before I could answer, he was headed toward the long-term parking shuttle. 'I'll call you.'

I turned back to Frank. 'My car's out here,' he said apologetically. I followed Frank out to his car parked in a fifteen-minute-limit spot outside baggage claim.

'How did you do this? There's no boot on your car; it hasn't been towed. There's no ticket. Even the Metro police chief got a ticket a few weeks ago for parking here barely over fifteen minutes.'

'The chief doesn't have as many friends on the force as I do,' Frank answered, laughing. 'These are airport police TSA employees, but this guy's a friend of mine; he's a Metro officer, just does this part time, on his days off from MNPD.'

He waved at the uniformed officer who made a show of putting away the ticket book he had been pretending to write in.

Frank loaded my luggage in his car and pulled out. I gave him directions to my house. He carried my bags inside, said he hoped the other guy looked worse, and left me standing in my living room with my tan fading faster than the bruises.

I listened to Maureen's message one more time and wished I had been here to hear what she had to say. Maybe if I had, she'd be alive today. I pulled out my phone and recorded Maureen's message to save.

FORTY-THREE

Sometime Monday Sam left a message on my voicemail at work asking how I was, but it was three days before I talked to him in person. I went to the small memorial service for Maureen Kennedy at Bitsy and Philip's church and thought I'd never seen sadder, more bewildered-looking people than Mr and Mrs Kennedy and the two Carter children.

Sam must have been behind me in the church because he was waiting outside when I came out.

'You OK?' he asked.

'I'm fine. Bruises are fading. Have you learned anything?'

'A little. You gonna be home tonight?' he asked. I nodded. 'I'll get by if I can. It may be late,' he warned. 'Just turn off your porch light if you're going to bed and don't want me to stop.'

'OK.' Yeah, like I was going to do that.

After Sam left, Philip Carter came over. 'Thanks for coming. I know the kids appreciate it. I mean, I appreciate it. We all do. But the children were especially close to Maureen. They've gone through so much. And the Kennedys, maybe it helps to know people over here cared about their daughter.'

I nodded. 'Sure. It's so sad. This must have been an expensive trip for them.'

'The Thompsons insisted on paying for it. Everett's probably thinking that's cheaper than a lawsuit.'

I didn't know what to say. That might be true, but it seemed a callous thing to say at Maureen's service. I stood there, feeling awkward, trying to think of something to say. 'How are Thompson and Rachel? It must have been awful for them.'

Philip sighed. 'They're tough kids. I mean it. I don't know how they do it. Rachel wanted to have a wake, a real Irish wake. Where she's even heard of that I don't know. But she got it in her mind that that's what Maureen would want and that it would make her parents feel better. Bitsy's parents were horrified. I think we're about to reenact the Troubles and the Post Office Uprising right here in Belle Meade. But Rachel won. Why don't you come by? We'll be at the Thompsons'.'

'Oh, I don't want to intrude.'

'Please. We need some real people. And you knew Maureen. I know some of her school friends will be there, but teenagers aren't the best at talking to adults sometimes. I think it would be good for the Kennedys to have someone to talk to besides Bitsy's parents.'

'Well, sure, if you think it would help.'

'Great. I'll see you there.'

Rachel met me at the door of her grandparents' house. 'Would you like some Irish whiskey?'

'I'm sorry?'

'Irish whiskey. You have to have whiskey at a wake, and I wanted it to be right. I looked it up.'

'Oh. That's very thoughtful of you. Thank you, but, no, thanks. Maybe some ice tea?'

'Of course. But you have to eat and drink. Maureen said that's what the Irish always do. And it's OK to cry and sing a song if it reminds you of Maureen.'

'Thank you. Rachel . . . If I don't sing a song, it's not because I don't care about Maureen. It's just that I'm not used to singing in front of people.'

'OK. Thank you for coming.' Rachel stood, formal and solemn, to welcome her other guests.

I found Maureen's parents in a corner with untouched glasses of whiskey, looking very uncomfortable.

'I'm so sorry about your daughter,' I said. 'Maureen was such a charming girl. I met her several times. I know you were proud of her.'

'That we were,' Mr Kennedy said stiffly. 'She was our youngest, mebbe the brightest of the lot.'

Mrs Kennedy started crying silently, tears just running down her face.

'These children certainly loved her,' I said. 'I hope you know that.'

Mrs Kennedy looked up then. 'Aye. Yer children there, they're angels, they are. Our Maureen loved them, too. Look at them, goin' t' all this trouble when their grandparents would sooner keep us in hidin' until they could ship us back. No, the wee ones are angels.'

'Did Maureen write to you much about things here in Nashville?'

'Sure and she did. She was always writin' us or emailin' to one of her brothers. We wouldn't know how to turn on one of them computers, me and Jack wouldn't, but Maureen, she was all modern 'n high tech. She told us enough. Enough to know somethin' wasn't right here. The master flirted with her, all right, but that's normal enough, I guess. She was a beautiful girl.' Mrs Kennedy fought to regain control. She got very quiet and still. 'It was t'other master she was afraid of, this Mr Thompson.'

'Do you know why?'

'Not precisely, no. But I know she thought all wasn't right between yer man and his daughter. She'd heard them fightin'. She said Miss Bitsy would be shakin' after, scared out of her wits.'

'Do you know what they argued about?'

'No, Maureen would be off with the children. Miss Bitsy wouldn't want them to hear. And they couldn't understand the words. But there was no mistakin' the shoutin'.'

I turned to look around the room and saw Mrs Thompson bearing down on us. I took a deep breath. 'Mrs Thompson. I know this must be difficult for you. It's kind of you to do this. It certainly seems to mean a lot to Rachel.'

'Yes. She's a strong-willed child. I'm glad you've met the Kennedys. Now, come have some refreshments. I see you managed to escape Rachel's whiskey.'

I looked back at the wilting Kennedys as I was being steered toward the dining room. 'I'm sorry.'

'Thank you,' Mrs Kennedy whispered.

'I don't want to be ungracious,' Mrs Thompson murmured into my ear, 'and goodness knows this is dreadful for those poor people, but really, if I'd known the kind of background these au pair girls come from. Superstitious, imaginative. I don't know that it would have made any difference, though. Bitsy is so headstrong.' Is, I noticed. 'I know you're busy, you won't have time to stay long, but do have some tea, a sandwich, something.'

Hint, hint?

Carrie shouldered her way through the swinging door carrying a large tray of finger sandwiches. Her eyes met mine, but neither of us said anything.

'Thanks, Mrs Thompson,' I said. 'I think I will have a glass of tea.'

'Yes, dear, do. I must go see about the children, but do.' She started away, then turned back. 'And thank you for coming, of course.'

I looked back at Carrie and raised my eyebrows. Carrie met my eyes with no expression on her face. She made a space for the tray, picked up another that was nearly empty and went back to the kitchen.

I picked up a glass of tea, bit into a truly delicious cream cheese and cucumber sandwich – that's a nearly lost art now – and looked around the room. Philip was talking to a couple of women whom I recognized as Bitsy's friends. Thompson was trying to entertain a cluster of red-eyed teenaged girls. A teenaged boy, good looking in a raw, gawky way sat by himself on the sofa.

I checked to make sure Mrs Thompson wasn't watching and went over to sit beside him. 'Hi. Friend of Maureen's?'

'Yeah.'

'From school?'

'Yeah.'

'I liked her,' I said. 'She always seemed to be a lot of fun.'

He looked at me, a fierce anger barely controlled in his face. 'She's the most wonderful woman I've ever known. I'll never forget her.'

I nodded. What could I say that wouldn't sound patronizing? This boy deserved better than that. I sat beside him for a while. Mrs Thompson hurried through the room, shot me a sharp look, but seemed reassured that I wasn't talking – or listening. I slipped a card out of my pocket once she was past. 'Look. I liked Maureen a lot. And I don't like that something happened to her. She called me a few days ago. I was out of town. I think she wanted to talk to me about something. How about giving me a call?'

He looked suspicious but took my card and stuck it in a pocket. 'Maybe.'

'What's your name?'

'Ryan. Ryan Sanders.' He told me he was from Nashville, that he'd grown up here, gone to Hillsboro to high school and just graduated last year.

'OK, Ryan. I'd like to talk to you. Your call.'

I thought about trying to talk to the girls but decided there would be no subtle way to do that. I said goodbye to Rachel and left. I went back to the office, but things were slow, it was nearly four, and I couldn't settle down. I checked my email, printed out a message from Sally O'Hara and went home.

FORTY-FOUR

At home I went to my room, kicked off my shoes, stripped off the pantyhose and funeral clothes and fell across the bed. I got up, put the tape with Maureen's message back in and listened one more time. She was afraid. She had something to tell me, and she was afraid for anyone else to know. I took the tape back out, popped in the new one and went to take a shower. I kicked my still packed suitcase as I walked by it.

I sure hoped Sam would make it by tonight. I needed to play Maureen's messsge for him, maybe let him make a copy of it.

I stood under the water and let it run hot. Why was she afraid? Was it for herself, or did she know something about Bitsy's disappearance? Had Philip's flirtation gotten out of hand? Was it Mr Thompson? She had schoolfriends, a boyfriend, apparently. Why had Maureen called me? And why hadn't I been there to listen?

My bruises were fading. But that yellow was not a becoming color for me. The warmth of the shower felt good, but even the water hurt my bruises. What was Captain Mick's problem? Did he know what had happened to Bitsy? Did he know the woman on his boat wasn't Bitsy Carter? And how would he have known that? And whom was he threatening, me or Sam?

From everything I had known, Mr Thompson was an indulgent father, paying for expenses, luxuries that his daughter and her husband couldn't afford. Why would he and Bitsy have argued so much and so loudly that an au pair experiencing America for the first time would have written home about that?

My head was going in circles and starting to hurt. I dried my hair, put on jeans and a flannel shirt and started the fire in my living room. It was still light out, but I made sure the porch light was on. Hot tea. Maybe a nap. I hadn't been through enough time zones to have jet lag, but I hadn't recovered from the trip. Maybe if I laid down here on the couch and rested my eyes a little, I'd feel better in a few minutes, fix some supper, figure out some of what was going on.

I woke to hear knocking. The house was dark except for the fire and the light from the porch light coming through the front windows. I felt disoriented. I had no idea what time it was. I opened the door, still rubbing my eyes. Sam was looking at his watch.

'I'm sorry,' he said. 'Were you asleep? I saw the porch light, thought you were expecting me.'

'What time is it?'

'Uhh . . . eight thirty. Look, I'm sorry. I'll talk to you tomorrow.' He was backing off the porch.

'No, no, come in. I just fell asleep on the couch. I meant for you to see the porch light on. Come on in.'

He did. I stumbled around, turned on a light. Maybe I should have left the lights off, more romantic. I was too tired to be romantic. And I was hungry.

'I'm hungry,' I said. 'Have you eaten?'

'No, but . . .'

I headed for the kitchen, Sam trailing behind. 'I'm starved. Let's see what I've got.' I hadn't been to the grocery store since I'd gotten home. There was no telling what was in the refrigerator and how many colors of mold were in there. I don't know what it is. You don't have to be gone long. You leave the house for a couple of days, and everything in your refrigerator thinks it's supposed to grow penicillin.

I had bread. Eggs, yeah, cheese. Not much else.

'Scrambled eggs, omelet or grilled cheese. Your choice.'

'No swordfish with caper sauce, lime remoulade?'

'Did you catch it and bring it in with you?'

'No amberjack with shrimp sauce?'

'Don't mess with the chef when she's hungry. You don't even have a choice of light bread or dark.'

'Grilled cheese.'

'All right. Coke?' I asked.

'Yeah, thanks,' he said. I took two cans out of the refrigerator along with butter and slices of American cheese. Sam opened the cans.

'So, what's new?' I melted butter in a sauté pan and put the cheese slices on wholewheat bread that I'd found in the freezer.

'Campbell, I know you're in the middle of this, but you know I can't give you confidential information from an ongoing investigation.'

'Yeah? I'll bet you're going to ask me if I've picked up anything.'

Sam was standing very close. 'Campbell . . .' He rubbed the back of my neck, then leaned over and kissed it lightly.

'Hey! I'm working with an open flame here.'

'Sorry. You do know it's a crime to withhold information relevant to a criminal investigation.'

'I'm just a civilian. What do *I* know? What makes you think I might know *anything*? What makes you think I might have been invited back to the Thompsons' house after the service? What makes you think I might have talked to Maureen's parents, met her boyfriend?'

'OK, OK. If any of this leaks to your newspaper buddy, I'll be an unemployed single father. Think about that.' He leaned back against the counter and stuck his hands in his pockets. 'We haven't found the homeless vet yet, but we will. He's been around town for decades; it's not likely that he's left now. But we don't think it matters much. We already have his prints to eliminate; we know where he told the minister he found the day planner. Not much more we're likely to learn from him. The Maury County coroner's report doesn't tell us much either. Maureen Kennedy died from fractured C1, C2 cervical vertebrae that resulted in a severed spinal cord. Your card was in her pocket. Death was instant. The diaphragm would have stopped immediately. You can't breathe, you die. The question is: what made her fall from that horse? Maury County Sheriff's Department didn't find any evidence that her tack had been tampered with. The farm manager had unsaddled the horse by the time they got there, but he showed it to them. Everything was in order. Could it have been loose? Maybe. No way to tell now. But Maureen was used to horses. She'd been riding since she was a child, so it's not likely she wouldn't have noticed that. And every-body agrees it was the farm manager who helped them saddle up, so, if he deliberately did something to her equipment, that's starting to look like a pretty wide conspiracy, and we don't think that's likely.'

'What about the children? What did they say happened?'

'They were a little ahead and not that close. They were racing, not too fast apparently, but spread out. Maureen was probably hanging back to keep an eye on them. It was a game they had. They'd race from a particular tree to a pond. Because of the trees, they'd spread out. Those kids have been riding all their lives, too.

'Thompson was the closest but he wasn't looking at Maureen; he was hanging on. He thinks he heard a loud noise, but isn't sure. Maybe a tree branch, maybe a shot. But she didn't die from a gunshot. She fell. They were all making a lot of noise, themselves. Thompson didn't think about it until investigators started asking, so maybe he's trying to give them what he thinks they want. We don't know. Could have been the horse was running, stepped on a fallen branch, lost its footing. That's the most likely thing. An accident. Things happen.'

'But people get thrown from horses all the time and get up and walk away.'

'Sure. But people die, too. You hit your head the wrong way, and your neck's broken,' Sam said.

I put the sandwiches on plates, added some grapes I found in the refrigerator. 'Get a couple of napkins, OK?'

Sam pulled a couple of paper towels off the roll. Close enough. We took dinner back to the living room couch.

'So what did the kids say happened next?'

'Maureen was lying there; the horse was stomping around, rearing. They rode for help.'

'How long would that have taken?'

'For them to ride back to the barn, get the manager's attention, for him to get on one of the Thompsons' horses and ride back? At least twenty minutes, maybe thirty or more.'

'And Maureen had died instantly?'

'Maureen died instantly when her neck was broken. The only real question is: was her neck broken instantly when she fell?'

'What do you mean?'

'Thirty minutes is a long time. Mr Thompson was at the house, never heard a thing.'

'Yeah?'

Sam shrugged, his mouth full of grilled cheese. 'This isn't in the official report, but one of the Maury County deputies told me there was mud on Mr Thompson's study floor. And mud on his shoe.'

'Mud. On a farm. In Tennessee,' I said flatly. 'That doesn't prove much.'

'Nope,' Sam agreed.

'Is that it?'

'Pretty much. I'm trying to get a line on our friend Mick Mikwozhewski. Called a friend with the FBI. That may take a while. I asked her to see what she could find on Sally O'Hara and Tom Cooper while she was at it.'

I nodded.

Sam prodded. 'Your turn.'

'OK. Listen to this.' I had told him Maureen had left me a message, but he hadn't heard it. I put the old tape in my answering machine, rewound it, pushed play, and turned up the volume. It was eerie listening to Maureen's voice after talking about her death. Her soft, Irish whisper filled the room.

'Miss Hale, don't call me back. Don't come to see me. I'll call you when I can.'

'Can I hang on to that?' Sam asked.

'Sure. Would you make me a copy? I don't know why, but I'd like to keep it.' I tried to think what other messages might be on that tape, messages I might not want the man who'd just kissed the back of my neck – or his work colleagues – to listen to. Oh, well, too late to tamper with the evidence now. 'Look, I'd appreciate it if the entire Metropolitan Nashville Police Department didn't listen to the rest of that tape.'

'Hmm. We'll see. What else? You've been home three days. Don't tell me you haven't been nosing around.'

'If some people want information that some people think other people might have, some people should be a little more polite to other people.'

'Run that by me again?'

'Never mind.' I handed him the printout of Sally O'Hara's email. None of the other passengers on the boat had admitted knowing either the woman who caught the marlin or Bitsy Thompson Carter. They did think the woman who fished with them seemed to know the captain, though. Sally had included their addresses and phone numbers. I decided Detective Davis and his staff could follow up on that.

'And the wake?'

'Oh, Sam, it was so sad. Those poor people.' I shook my head. 'Maureen wrote home often. She wrote letters to her

parents and emails to her brothers. She wrote about the Carters and the Thompsons, said Philip flirted with her, but the mother didn't seem too concerned about that, seemed to think it was normal, didn't mean anything; Maureen was prepared for it, it hadn't gone anywhere.' Sam nodded. 'But Mrs Kennedy said Mr Thompson was another matter. The Thompsons paid for the Kennedys to fly over, by the way. Maureen had said that he and Bitsy argued, often and violently, well, loudly, at least. Maureen and the kids would be in another part of the house, but they'd hear the shouting. Mrs Kennedy suggested Maureen was afraid of him.' I stopped. 'Come to think of it, I've always been a little afraid of him, but not like I think he's going to murder me, just . . . intimidated, I guess.'

Sam shrugged. 'OK, a father and daughter argued. A father who paid a lot of his adult, married daughter's expenses.'

'Yeah. And there was the boyfriend.'

'Maureen's boyfriend?'

'Well, I don't really know how serious it was. A boy. Heartbroken. I don't know how Maureen felt, but he was in love with her. Ryan Sanders. From the community college where she studied part-time. There were some girls there, too. They might be worth talking to. I thought I could probably get their names from Ryan.'

'*You* could get their names from Ryan?'

'I gave him my card. I figured he wouldn't be too hard to find even if he doesn't call.'

Sam leaned over and touched a fading, yellow bruise. 'See that? That's why you're not supposed to go asking strangers questions.'

'And I thought you were supposed to protect me,' I said lightly and knew immediately that was a mistake.

Sam scowled. 'Yeah. I guess I wasn't too good at that. I knew better. I should never have let you go down there.'

'Let me go?' Sam didn't seem to hear the dangerous calm in my own voice.

'Yeah. It won't happen again.'

'Really?'

Sam stood up and carried his can and our empty plates to

the kitchen. 'I'd better go. I haven't been home much.' I
followed, seething, with our paper towels and my own can.
'Thanks for supper. You make a good grilled cheese.'

'Well, I'm good in the kitchen.'

'Yeah, you are.' He was oblivious, thinking he was
complimenting me.

Barefoot, I followed him to the door.

'I'll call,' he said.

I nodded grimly.

He kissed my forehead and left. I slammed the door.

FORTY-FIVE

On my way to work the next day, I went by to see
Charlie at AAAAuto. 'How you doin', Miz Hale?'

'Good, Charlie, how about you?'

'Not bad for the shape I'm in. Got those carburetors in.
They were in good shape. Fit just fine. I'm still looking for a
crank case. Body work's looking good. We'll paint it before
long.'

'I appreciate it, Charlie. I'm going to write you a check
today.'

He waved away any concern about something as crass as
money where a classic Spider was involved. 'Time enough
when I've got 'er runnin'.'

I insisted, and he said I could write a check for the cost of
the carburetors. I added a hundred dollars, the total still less
than he'd already spent on parts. I folded the check and handed
it to him.

'Any word on Miz Bitsy?'

'Nothing. Nothing that seems to help.' I gave him an
abbreviated report on my trip to Mexico and the wake.

He shook his head. 'It's a shame, but I could have told you
she didn't park that Spider of hers in airport parking and leave
town. Miz Bitsy would not have treated that car that way. No
offense, Miz Hale, but she takes better care of hers than you

do of yours. I know you ain't got no garage to put yours in ev'ry night, but Miz Bitsy's never sat out overnight. She never left it in the weather. She wouldn't 'a done that. She'd 'a taken a taxi first.'

Taxi.

When I got to the office, I called Sam and asked him to take me to lunch.

He seemed a little surprised. 'Well, sure, OK, if I can get away.'

'I need to talk to you about something.'

'OK. I'll call you back a little later.'

By the time Sam called back later that morning, I had flipped through the *Tennessean*. There was a home baseball game at Lipscomb.

'I can make it if a late lunch is OK. Maybe one thirty?'

'That's fine.' I was easy. 'And we can go to your favorite place.'

'My favorite place?'

'The baseball field. Lipscomb.'

'All right.' There was more enthusiasm in his voice now. 'I'll see you there. One thirty.'

FORTY-SIX

The day was chillier than the first game we'd been to, but sunny, and I had a blanket in the car. Sam had one, too, plus a couple of stadium cushions. 'When you have a daughter who's a cheerleader,' he explained, 'you have to stay prepared for athletic events in any weather conditions.' This time we had hot chocolate with our hot dogs.

The crowd was small and quieter than before. The Lipscomb left fielder hit a home run, but the applause was muffled by mittens and gloves.

'We've talked to most everyone who was on the fishing boat,' Sam said. 'There doesn't seem to be any link. The only thing interesting was that some of them did think the woman called Bitsy seemed to know the captain. Mrs Luke? From Mississippi? She said they kept touching each other, trying to make it look accidental.' He shrugged. 'We're still working on Captain Mick.'

I told Sam about Charlie, how incredulous he'd been when I had first told him about Bitsy's car being left in long-term parking. 'The thing is, if Bitsy never went to Mexico, how did her car get there? Somebody else had to drive it, and that somebody else had to get back home somehow.'

'Yeah.'

'There might be something on security cameras. And taxis.'

'We showed Bitsy's picture around to taxi drivers,' Sam said.

'Right. But this wouldn't be Bitsy. This would be whoever wanted to make it look like she had disappeared.'

'Yeah, OK.' Sam was thinking. 'It's been so long now, though, it's not likely any driver's going to remember a face. But we can get the destinations. We know from the parking ticket when the car was left there, so that narrows down the information we need from the taxi companies. Yeah.'

He pulled out his phone and made a call. Frank or someone like him would be calling taxi operators before the inning was over.

Sam turned to me. 'We have a budget, you know, for paying informants. Want another cup of hot chocolate?'

FORTY-SEVEN

I worked hard that day. Except for fifty minutes of NCAA baseball, I worked really hard. But part of the time that I was working I was on hold with a cruise line or tour company; I was standing at the fax machine; I was copying destination information for a client. And all the time I was thinking. Who could I talk to about Bitsy's relationship with her father? Not Philip. And certainly not Mrs Thompson. Whatever sleeping dogs were in that household, she was taking

very good care to make sure they could lie undisturbed. The children, no. That wouldn't be right. Besides, they probably wouldn't know anything more than Maureen had. I thought about Bitsy's friends, but if I talked to them it would probably get back to Bitsy's family.

Carrie Johnson.

I didn't know her phone number or her husband's name, but I knew where she lived. I had taken her home. If she was listed, I could narrow it down. After that, whenever I was on hold, I was looking through the Nashville phone book listings for Johnsons. There are five pages of Johnsons in the Nashville book. Five pages, four columns each, of very small print. Somewhere around two thousand residential listings for Johnsons. And none for the address I had taken Carrie to. But the second time through, I found one that had to be nearby. Across the street and a house or two down. And likely to know Carrie, a neighbor with the same last name. Might even be a relative if I was lucky. I called, but no answer. Maybe later. I'd try after I got home.

FORTY-EIGHT

A t seven thirty that night, I was in luck. Abner Johnson did indeed know Carrie, his sister-in-law, who lived catty-cornered across the street, and he gave me her phone number. I called and found her at home.

'I don't think I know nothin' that would help you. They never was particularly close, not like Miss Bitsy and her mother. He bought her anything she wanted, but he never seemed to show her affection, if you know what I mean. 'Course, him not bein' her real father, I always thought it was that.'

'Not her real father?'

'Well, not exactly. He's the only father she's ever known, and, as far as I know, she's never known any different. But Miz Thompson was already in the fam'ly way when she and

Mr Thompson married. Not too far along, and she didn't go out right after Bitsy was born, not for about three months or so, so she let on Miss Bitsy's birthday was about ten weeks later than it actually was. Then said the baby was premature. That was supposed to be why she didn't go out, the doctor was afraid she might lose the baby so she had to lie flat on her back.

'She'd been seein' Mr Thompson and her family wanted her to marry him, but she thought she was in love with another boy, nobody disgraceful, just an ordinary boy, not in college, in the service. Somebody whose father had worked for her family down at the farm. That farm was in her family, you know. Then after he'd been home on leave she was expectin', thinkin' her parents would have to let her marry him now. Mr Thompson worked in the bank then, didn't have the money her family did, but he was from a good family. The boy got killed overseas, and before long his family was gone, too. They tried to send Miz Thompson to Chicago to get rid of the baby, but she refused, said she'd kill herself if they tried to make her. I guess that's where Miss Bitsy got her stubbornness. Miz Thompson just used up all she had on keepin' that baby.

'Mr Thompson didn't go anywhere, said he still wanted to marry her. I don't know. I think it was the money. Now Mr Thompson's made a lot of money, but the real money's in Miss Bitsy's name, bank stock and land and all, tied up in some trust fund, from Mrs Thompson's family. I think it was to be divided between all the chirren they had, but they never was any more. Just Miss Bitsy. I think Miz Thompson's daddy wanted to make sure Miss Bitsy wouldn't be treated any different than any later chirren.'

I thought.

'Carrie,' I said suddenly. 'One more thing. I've heard some rumors that Bitsy had a lover? Do you know anything about that?'

'No,' she answered without hesitating. 'I wouldn't blame her too much, though. She's worth a hundred of Mr Philip, but I never seen anything that would make me think that.' She was silent for a few minutes. 'You know, I never told any of

this before, not in all these years, but I'm worried to death about Miss Bitsy. If this helps you find her, so be it. They find out and let me go, I'll just get that job at Walmart.'

I decided to try Mark. I didn't think he'd still be at the paper this late. His deadline was usually early afternoon. No answer at home, but I left a message on his cell phone.

An hour later, the phone rang. 'What's up?' It was Mark.

'Suppose the Thompson family fortune was really locked up somehow, in a trust, say, where Everett Thompson had only limited control, maybe just the income, say?'

'Well,' Mark said, 'just supposing, that could make it tough for him under certain conditions, say big market losses, or a real estate venture that didn't pay off like that big downtown condominium conversion that never got off the ground. He invested big in that, I heard, and Nashville didn't seem to be ready for downtown luxury condominiums at the time. Not at the price they were planning on asking, anyway. If he borrowed to invest in that, he could be hurting to pay back the loans. I'll ask around. It'll probably be tomorrow, though, before I'll have anything.'

'Thanks.'

'No problem.'

I was already in bed, just turning off the news when the phone rang again. 'Hello.'

It was Sam. 'You see, the reason you have to have the infield fly rule is that . . .'

'Wimpy, wimpy rule. It would never happen in football. Sorry,' I said sarcastically, 'if you make an interception on a third down in the fourth quarter facing the wind on the left side of the field, you lose six points. Wouldn't happen. You play the game. You blitz, you might get sucked into an option. It's the chance you take.'

'Are you kidding me? Don't play rough with the kicker. You'll get a penalty for that. Quarterback's are special. Don't hit them late, another penalty. Baseball's a real game. A man's game.' His voice changed, serious now. 'How are the bruises?'

'About gone.'

'We're working the taxi angle. Nothing yet. Lot of taxis go through the airport in a couple of hours.'

'I have something else.'

'What do you mean you have something else? You're not supposed to "have something". You're supposed to let the police do their job, do our job. My job.'

'Fine,' I said.

'Good.'

'Absolutely,' I agreed. I waited. Silence. 'So you don't want to know what else I have?'

'What?' He sounded a little angry.

'It might be nothing, but it's interesting. I might know a little more tomorrow.'

Sam groaned. 'What?'

'Everett Thompson.'

'You told me. They argued. Lots of parents and children argue. I sometimes argue with my daughter. What kind of father murders his own daughter?'

'He's not her father. Everett Thompson is not Bitsy's father.'

'What?' It was a different what. I had his attention, at least. I told him what Carrie had said. He listened.

'OK. Doesn't prove a thing, but we'll look into it. We, the police, will look into it.'

'Good. And I'll let you know what else I find out.'

'Campbell!'

I didn't say anything. He didn't say anything. He sighed. 'I'll call you. Goodnight.' We were a long way from Mexico.

FORTY-NINE

The very next day, one of my favorite clients called, Agnes Elliston. Agnes was eighty-seven and determined to go full speed as long as she lived. 'I've decided to write my memoirs, Campbell. I'm afraid if I don't get started soon I won't have time to get finished. Find me someplace quiet I can go to write. I can't concentrate here. There's always too much going on.'

'Warm or cold?' I asked.

'Warm. Sun. And good food.'

'I've got the place for you.' I told Agnes about Spa Quetzalcoatl. I told her about the *casita* with the skylights and Zihuatanejo and Jésus and Manuel and the reflexology – and the food.

'Fine,' she said. 'Book me. Next week.'

'That's where Bitsy Carter is supposed to have gone.'

Agnes was a member of the Club herself. A Lady Member, actually. There's a special category for widows or other unmarried women. Agnes has been campaigning to change that for the last sixty years, first before she married, later after her husband died. She may be the Club's only women's rights activist. She's rich enough, old enough and related to enough of the members that they tolerate her, but change comes slowly at the Club.

'Poor Bitsy. She was a friend of yours, wasn't she?' Agnes asked.

'Yes.' Was.

'Always such a bright child. That's not always an advantage, you know. Her mother would have been better off to have brazened it out.'

'You knew?'

'My dear child, I know everything in this town. Well, not all the new people, of course,' she said, dismissing anyone with fewer than four generations of Nashville history. 'Hardly anybody else knew, though, although there are always whispers when a premature baby looks as big and healthy as Bitsy did. Most people thought Everett had just gotten a little impatient. Evelyn had her own money, though. She could have gone anywhere, done anything she wanted.'

'Unless what she wanted was to fit in here – or for her daughter to.'

Agnes sighed. 'Yes, of course. I used to wonder what would have happened if that boy had come back. I think he'd have given Evelyn backbone. Who knows? What else do I need to know about this spa?'

'Not much. I'll book it and get back to you. They'll pick you up at the airport.'

'We'll see. I may want to rent a little convertible.' That's Agnes.

My friend MaryNell called about eleven. 'Do you have time for lunch?' she asked. 'I want the scoop on the Mexico trip.'

'I don't. Not that I don't look forward to being grilled.'

MaryNell laughed. 'OK. But soon.'

'Soon,' I agreed. 'Hey, does Melissa have friends at Nashville State?'

'I don't know. I'll ask her. Why?'

I told MaryNell about Maureen Kennedy and the grief-stricken boy. 'I don't want to scare him, but I'd sure like to talk to him.'

'We play Hillsboro tomorrow night. Want to go?'

'Yeah, yeah, I will.'

Mark called that afternoon. 'You're right. Everett Thompson's credit's stretched about as far as it can go, and most of the family money is tied up. It's complicated. If Bitsy Carter's really dead, a lot of lawyers are going to be busy for a while figuring out who gets the money. Nobody's seen her will, of course, but the whole estate is . . . complicated. Some of it will go to Philip Carter and their children, but some of it will revert to Evelyn Thompson, which means Everett will have access to it to pay off his creditors. But if nobody's found, it'll be a while before that happens. It'll be interesting.'

'Yeah, thanks.'

'So what happened in Mexico?' Mark asked.

I told him what we'd found, what we hadn't found. I told him about my bruises and Captain Mick.

'I'll do some checking myself. See what I can find. But what I really meant was, what happened in Mexico?'

'Oh.' Sometimes I wished my friends weren't quite so interested. 'Nothing happened in Mexico. Nothing was supposed to happen in Mexico.'

'I'm sorry.' He didn't sound sorry. He sounded as if he were laughing.

FIFTY

Outside in Hillsboro Village, in spite of the day's chill, I could tell spring was coming. The sky seemed lighter as I drove home. I liked watching the days getting longer. I was driving home to a Friday night alone and wishing I had that one last day in Mexico, watching a long sunset from a mountaintop.

I was sitting on 440 just before the Nolensville Road exit when I thought, I don't have to go home and spend Friday night alone. When I had inched up enough that I could, I took the exit at Nolensville Road, headed south to Thompson Lane and went back west. At Hillsboro Road, I turned left toward Green Hills and an art gallery that carried a few of Bitsy's pieces. It seemed like the place I could be closest to her, and only Bitsy had the answers now.

There were just two cars in the parking lot. It was too late for daytime shoppers, too early for after-dinner browsers. Inside there was just one person besides one of the owners. The owner gave me an exhibit guide. 'Is there anything in particular I can show you?'

'No, thanks. I just want to look around.'

'Great. There's some wine, bottled water, cheese. Help yourself.' She smiled and went back to her desk.

The only other person was a man. Forty, maybe forty-five. Medium height, short dark hair. Khakis and a sport jacket. MaryNell was always telling me I should get out more. Maybe this was what she meant. The thing was, I had come here to think about Bitsy. I had been in the studio with her when she was working on two of the pieces on display here. I wanted to look at them, be alone with . . . I don't know what, memories, thoughts.

And this man was standing right in front of the pedestal that held my favorite, a larger, more elaborate version of the vase Bitsy had given me. It was over two feet tall, and flowers

and ferns seemed to grow out of the vase itself. The colors in
the clay, fired and matte glazed now, were earthy, woodsy
colors, the colors of roots and bulbs and new growth in old
leaves. It made me want to touch it, just the way it had that
afternoon in Bitsy's studio.

I wandered around, looking at other pieces. Bitsy's were
the only clay works here. There were paintings by three artists,
and a collection of textiles, some pieces mounted, some shawls,
scarves and jackets to wear. Beautiful, glowing colors painted
on raw silk. It made me feel rested, peaceful. But the man
stayed there by Bitsy's vase. Finally, as I circled, I saw tears
in his eyes. Now, I like a man to be sensitive, appreciate art,
but this seemed a little extreme.

Afraid of intruding, I moved back to the other side of the
display space, near the desk. The owner looked up, smiling.
I inclined my head toward the man, not wanting to say anything
to draw his attention. I raised my eyebrows, asking the woman
a silent question. She looked, shrugged. 'He's been here several
times lately,' she whispered.

I nodded and moved away, waiting until he moved.

Finally, he came over to the desk.

'I'd like to buy that vase,' he said. 'The tall one, there.'

He was buying Bitsy's vase. My vase! He'd stood in front
of it so I couldn't stand there myself, think about her in private,
and now he was buying it. And that made me curious.

I browsed while he made the purchase.

'Would you like it delivered?' the woman asked.

'No, I'll take it with me.'

'Fine. Would you mind filling this out?'

'No, I don't want to be on a mailing list or anything. I just
want to buy the vase.'

'OK. Sure. Of course.' She processed the man's credit card
and gave him the ticket to sign. 'I'll just pack it for you.' I
tried to see his signature, but I couldn't read it.

She took the vase carefully from its pedestal and carried it
to a back room. That meant I was alone with the man.

'I like her work, too,' I offered.

He nodded. Closed, no tears now. Nothing.

'Do you have any other pieces of hers?'

'No.'

'I have a small vase that's similar to that one, just . . . smaller.' I held my hands up to measure eight inches or so. 'She's a friend of mine.' I watched his face closely, and I saw pain, pure and raw. It hit me suddenly that I had not seen that kind of pain on Philip Carter's face since Bitsy had been gone. Not on anyone's face except her children. 'You . . .' I didn't know what I was going to say. You're the lover?

'Look,' I said, 'she really is a friend of mine. I'm Campbell Hale. Can we talk?'

He started shaking his head.

'Please. Just a few minutes. Let's get a cup of coffee somewhere. Please.'

The owner came back with a large box, which she set on her desk. She folded the credit receipt and put it into a gallery envelope. 'Thank you,' she said. 'Please come again. We have new exhibits every month.'

He nodded, then looked at me. 'OK,' he said, and I followed him out.

Outside, I asked, 'Starbucks?'

He shrugged. 'Yeah.'

A few blocks away the man waited at the coffee shop door and held it open for me. 'What do you drink?'

'Just coffee, cream.'

'No latte, cappuccino, frappé whatever?'

'Just coffee.'

He nodded.

He brought two cups of coffee back to the table where I waited and sat down. He was nearly as tall as Sam, and his skin had the weathered look of a man who works outside.

I didn't know what to say, where to start. So that's what I said. 'I don't know what to say, but Bitsy Carter is a friend of mine. I, uh, I want to know what's happened to her.' He started backing away, his jaw tightening. 'No, no, I don't mean I think you did anything. I just think, thought, I mean, when you were in the gallery, well, I thought you must know her, too, and . . . and . . . care about her.'

'I can't help you. I don't know anything. I didn't even know she was going to Mexico. If she was planning a trip, she didn't tell me.'

'Would she? Have told you, I mean?'

'I thought so.'

'Were you . . . I mean, were you and Bitsy . . .?'

I saw the first hint of a smile. 'No. We weren't. But I thought we might be, someday. There were some things she had to sort out.'

'Philip.'

He inclined his head.

'Was she going to divorce Philip?'

'She was trying to be fair to him, fair to that jerk. He'd been messing around on her for years. But, you know, the kids, and all. She wanted them to tell the kids together. It wasn't about me, she said.' He shrugged. 'I was ready to wait. I *was* waiting.'

'Did anybody know about . . . you and Bitsy?'

The almost smile again, but sad. 'There really wasn't a me and Bitsy yet, but no, except maybe the nanny, au pair, whatever.'

'Maureen.'

He nodded.

'Who died a few days ago.'

He nodded.

'How do you know Bitsy?'

'I'm a builder.' He shrugged. 'One of my crews was remodeling her house.' He turned the cup in his hand. 'She made me coffee.' As if that explained it.

I sat there and thought for a few minutes. He sat and drank his coffee. Bitsy, who in an odd way controlled the financial destiny of too many people to whom money meant too much, was planning to divorce Philip. And she wanted to tell him before she talked to anyone else about it. Nobody knew except this sad man across from me who looked just like that seventeen-year-old boy I had seen on the Thompsons' sofa. Like he'd lost everything. I took a deep breath and told him all about Mexico. Well, not all about Mexico, of course, just the part about Bitsy or, rather, not Bitsy. I didn't repeat anything I knew from Sam, just what I'd found out on my own.

His expression never changed. 'I hope you figure it out,' he said. 'If somebody hurt her, I hope the police find him and put him away, but, you know, it doesn't bring her back. I don't care about justice. I just want Bitsy.'

I nodded. 'Do you mind telling me your name?' I'd already written down his car license tag number and a description of the car. I figured I could get the credit card number from the gallery owner – or Sam could. One way or another, I knew I could track him down.

He extended his hand across the table. 'Dan Neal. Any friend of Bitsy's is a friend of mine.'

Dan Neal: d n.

I shook his hand. 'Likewise.'

He took a deep breath. 'I've tried to stay quiet, stay out of this because I didn't want to embarrass Bitsy or her family.' He shrugged. 'I didn't really know anything.' He got up and started for the door. He turned back. 'I'm glad you spoke. It's good to talk about her.' And he left.

Could I get hold of Sam? Of course, not.

FIFTY-ONE

I had a lot to think about on the drive home. And by then I was hungry.

I got off I-40 at Donelson Pike, where I had my choice of America's finest fast food restaurants. Not to mention airport area motels and hotels. If I wanted to leave a car at the airport, make it look like someone had driven there and flown out, where would I have my own car stashed?

I got a cheeseburger, Ched'R'Peppers, and a lemonade at Sonic and turned around to cruise back along Donelson Pike to the airport. I turned in and drove by the terminal on the ground transportation level. I circled again on the baggage claim level. I went slowly and paid attention to the hotel shuttles. Holiday Inn, a Holiday Inn Express, Hampton Inn, Hilton, Sheraton, Embassy Suites, Marriott, Wyndham, and more. I exited back onto Donelson Pike and drove by several of the hotels. Not the Sheraton or the full-service Marriott, I thought. There, bellmen would notice if whoever dropped off Bitsy's car at the airport got off the shuttle but didn't go inside and check in. A smaller hotel, then, large enough to have regular shuttle service and be busy. He wouldn't have wanted to be the only one on the shuttle. Unless he took a taxi, but a shuttle made more sense, more anonymous. But a hotel or motel small enough not to have bell service. Small enough that he could have gone into the lobby, maybe gone to a phone or rest room, then back out to the parking lot without anyone noticing.

I circled the hotel areas off Donelson Pike and Elm Hill Pike. There would have been no point in going further away than that. More time, more chance of being seen. No, he had to have left his car in one of these dozen or so hotel parking lots. I looked for security cameras in the parking lots and made a list.

It wasn't until I was heading home that I remembered the day planner. Someone had thrown Bitsy's day planner into a dumpster in Donelson, a dumpster near the church where the homeless veteran had gone for a meal and a warm place to sleep. I turned around in the church parking lot. Which hotel was the closest? That would be the most logical place to start.

I tried to reach Sam again. Still no answer. So I left a message. 'You're the professional, I know. But I had a thought. If whoever left Bitsy's Spider in the airport lot also threw away her day planner, you might start from that end. Checking hotels closest to the church where the day planner was.' I told him which two I'd check first. 'And I know who "d n" is.' Then I went home.

FIFTY-TWO

On Saturday morning, I went to the grocery store. I finally unpacked. I did laundry; I cleaned the kitchen. I made a pot of chili big enough to last me long after I was tired of it. A little more laundry, a shower, and MaryNell was there to pick me up for the basketball game.

'I asked Melissa if she knew many kids at Nashville State,' MaryNell reported. 'Not a lot, she said. A few kids she's been in school with, a couple of girls she's played AAU ball with. She said she'd ask around. A lot of Nashville kids go there. They have a surprising number of international students, too. Now, Mexico?'

I filled MaryNell in. 'Well, hey, you have to respect that,' she said when I told her about Sam's contract with his daughter. 'Good kisser, though?'

I changed the subject.

We were early, and there were few spectators in the new Hillsboro gym. The nearly empty gym reflected the sounds of balls bouncing as the girls shot warm-up baskets, the squeak of basketball shoes on a polished floor. Cheerleaders started to arrive, line up their pom-poms, practice their cheers in odd little half motions. Julie saw me and waved. I waved back.

After the game started, there was more noise: officials' whistles, players yelling warnings, coaches shouting, cheerleaders' chants. The gym was starting to fill. Sam came in and spoke to his daughter. She said something and pointed toward where MaryNell and I sat. He came over.

'Hello,' he said as he sat down beside me.

'Hi.'

'Hey, Sam,' MaryNell greeted him.

'How you doing?'

'Good. You?'

'Fine,' Sam replied.

MaryNell wasn't through. 'Nice tan.'

Sam nodded and grinned. 'I got your message,' he said to me.

There was a sudden stir in the small crowd. The head coach of the University of Tennessee Lady Vols had come into the gym. She sat across from us.

'Who's she looking at, MaryNell?' I asked. The Lady Vols are perennial national championship contenders in women's basketball. Usually assistant coaches scouted, sitting anonymously in quiet upper corners of gyms. It was a little unusual to see a head coach, and she was attracting attention.

'Nobody on our team,' MaryNell answered sadly. 'I guess it's the Hillsboro post player. She's really good.'

The coach seemed oblivious to the attention around her. She was watching the game.

I turned back to Sam. 'Any luck yet?'

'We're going through the security tapes. It's a matter of time now. We got some information that someone bought a driver's license here in Nashville with the name Mary Elizabeth T. Carter about six weeks ago. Somebody sent what the guy was pretty sure was a valid license along with a new photograph for him to add to it, a woman who looked a lot like the original.'

'Can the guy who made the license identify the person who brought it in?'

'That would be nice. No. The money – cash, license, and photo were left in a drop box. The new license was mailed to a post office box. Guy didn't keep a record. People in his line of work tend not to. And his clients tend to be shy.'

'How did you find this out? Did you arrest the guy?'

'Informant. And, no, we didn't arrest anybody. No evidence. We could probably go in and find enough to shut him down, but not for long. And the next time there wouldn't be any information.'

'There's something else.' I told him about Dan Neal.

'How do you do this? You do realize that if Bitsy Carter is dead, someone around her is a murderer? You can't just go off with strange men.'

Except for that trip to Zihuatanejo, I thought.

'I went to Starbucks! In my own car!' I pulled the scrap of paper with Dan Neal's license plate number and my scribbled description of his car out of my purse and handed it to Sam. 'Here.'

Sam raised his eyebrows.

'His license plate.'

'OK.' He sighed. 'Thanks.'

'She was going to leave Philip.'

He nodded. 'Maybe. You know, you've just ruined my Saturday night. I'd better get somebody checking on this. I'll call you when I can. Be careful. MaryNell, see you.'

'Yeah, nice to see you, Sam.'

'Bye.' I watched him go, stopping to speak to his daughter on his way out. She nodded and turned back to the game. Maybe I could have waited to the end of the game.

I alternated watching the game and scanning the growing crowd. Finally, just before the end of the third quarter, I saw Ryan Sanders. I'd wondered if he might show up. After all, he'd been in school here last year, and Nashville State had no basketball team, no new draw for his loyalty. He was sitting with a small group of boys, but he was apart. They were laughing and talking; he was silent. Once in a while, one of the boys would say something to him, punch him in the shoulder. He'd respond, but he wasn't having fun.

When I saw him get up and move toward the concession stand, I followed.

I managed to get behind him in line. 'Ryan.'

He turned, didn't recognize me at first, then did. A guarded look closed his face.

'I'm here because a friend plays for McGavock, but you're right. I want to talk to you.'

'Why should I talk to you? You're not the police.'

'You want to talk to the police? I have a friend who is. I can call him right now.' I didn't want that to sound like a threat. I tried to make it sound like an option.

'No. I don't want to talk to anybody.'

'Look, I just want to know if Maureen had talked to you about what was going on with the Carters, the Thompsons.'

'Sure. She talked about them all the time. And she's dead.'

'Yes. I'm really sorry. I liked Maureen. But if she told you something that might make a difference . . .'

Ryan Sanders stared into my eyes. His silence stretched. 'It's too late. Mrs Carter's dead. Maureen's dead.'

'How do you know Mrs Carter's dead?'

'Everybody knows Mrs Carter's dead. Where would she be?'

'What did Maureen know? Did Maureen talk about Mrs Carter having a friend? A man?'

He shrugged. 'She didn't know anything. She didn't even know anything, and he killed her.'

'Who killed her?'

He looked away. 'Whoever she talked to.'

'Ryan, if you're right, there's a murderer loose. And if he killed Bitsy and then Maureen, don't you see? Somebody has to stop him! You have to trust somebody. I can put you in touch with the police. No one has to know. You can trust Detective Davis.'

'No.'

'Then tell me! Tell me what you know or what you heard. What Maureen thought, what she saw.'

Ryan's face changed, and I knew I had hit on it. Maureen had seen something that made her suspect someone. And, unless her death was a horrible coincidence, it looked like she had been right.

Ryan Sanders turned to the concessions counter and ordered his hot dog and coke. He paid, picked up his snacks, and waited while I ordered and paid for two cokes. I followed him to the table set up for mustard, ketchup and relish. He squirted mustard on his hot dog and made up his mind. 'It was something to do with Mrs Carter's studio. Nobody used that studio except Mrs Carter. And after she was gone, just a few nights after, someone was messing around in the studio late one night.'

'Well, that could mean nothing. Mr Carter could have gone out there looking for something.'

'Yeah. Right. She couldn't tell who was in there, but from Maureen's window she can see in the studio skylights. Somebody put something in the kiln, Mrs Carter's kiln, and left it on all night. She was talking to me on the phone. They didn't turn on the lights in the studio, but she could see enough to know they—'

I interrupted. 'They, more than one?'

'No, no, just one person. Anyway, he, she, whatever, put some stuff in the kiln and turned it on. When it's on, this red light glows until it's cool. Then a green light comes on.' I nodded. I had seen what he was describing. The green light meant it was safe to open the kiln. 'Maureen can see the light from her window. At night, I mean. The red light came on. Whoever it was sneaked out, and the light stayed on all night. Well, until Maureen went to sleep, at least.'

'What happened next? Did Maureen hear anyone come into the house? Like Mr Carter?'

'Nope. Nothing. Mr Carter wasn't there. He went to a dinner meeting. He came in a couple of hours later. She saw his car pull in and heard him come in the house, but she didn't talk to him.'

'Did Maureen ever say if she knew who had keys to the studio?'

'That night, while we were talking, she said there was a key hidden under a pot beside the studio door.'

'So most anyone could have known.'

Ryan nodded. 'That's all I know. Except it kept bothering Maureen, and now she's dead.'

I let Ryan go back to his friends, and I took a coke back to MaryNell. I wished Sam were still here.

FIFTY-THREE

It was still early when MaryNell dropped me off. A message from Mark said an Alfred R. Mikwozhewski had graduated from MIT the same year as Philip Carter. The roommate? 'He developed and patented a navigational gizmo that had made him a small fortune. He sold the engineering firm he owned five years later and moved to Mexico. The MIT alumni office had a post office box address in Tijuana, but they were afraid it wasn't current. They would be delighted to have an updated address for Mr Mikwozhewski.'

The answer was in Bitsy's studio, or it had been a few weeks ago. If I could go sometime when Philip wasn't there and look around for . . . What? I didn't know what I was looking for, so how would I know if I found it?

I looked at my watch. Just nine o'clock. I wasn't a total idiot, though. I wasn't going to charge over there by myself and start looking around at what might be a murder scene without some kind of backup. Maybe Philip had been gone that night, but I wasn't going to take any chances on running into him. I pressed the numbers on my phone to keep my name and number from showing up on caller ID and called Philip and Bitsy's number.

'Hello.' Philip Carter's voice. Not tonight. I hung up.

An hour or so later, I heard a knock at the door. Sam.

'Hi,' I said as I opened the door.

'Hi. Who won the game?'

'Hillsboro.'

Sam nodded and followed me into the den.

'Have you found out anything?'

'We found your buddy Dan Neal.'

'And?'

'I don't see that he had anything to gain by killing her. Could always have been a crime of passion; he wanted her to leave her husband, but she wouldn't. We'll keep an eye on him. We didn't learn anything except that he doesn't think she disappeared on her own.'

I nodded. Although I was convinced that Dan Neal had already told me everything he knew. I stood there waiting for Sam to thank me. It didn't happen.

Sam tilted his head, and his eyes caught the light. Clear and blue, they seemed to shine. 'Got an extra Coke?'

I realized it was the first time we'd been alone since Mexico. I was suddenly nervous. Mexico hadn't resolved our relationship; it had only complicated it more. 'Yeah. Sure.'

He followed me to the kitchen, leaning carelessly against the counter while I found Cokes in the refrigerator, put ice in glasses. Still leaning, he moved closer, watching while I poured the drinks, found napkins.

'I, uh, I talked to Maureen's boyfriend at the ballgame,' I told him.

He closed his eyes for a second and took a deep breath. He reached out and tucked a loose strand of hair behind my ear, his fingers lightly brushing my face. He didn't say anything.

I swallowed, not sure what to say, what to do. 'He thinks Maureen knew something. But after Bitsy disappeared, not before.'

Sam slammed his hand against the kitchen counter. 'Can we not spend *five minutes* together talking about something, *anything*, but a murder?' he yelled. 'Is there anything *wrong* with that?'

I jumped, shocked. My mouth dropped open. I'd never heard Sam raise his voice before. I shook one of the glasses, spilled some Coke. I reacted, reached for a paper towel and knocked over the glass.

'Oh, man!' Sam ripped some paper towels off the roll. I was scrambling to right the glass, but somehow it rolled off the counter. We both tried to catch it at the same time, banged our heads into each other and missed the glass. It hit the floor and exploded. Coke and shards of glass went everywhere. I was barefoot.

'*Don't move!*' he yelled. '*Don't move!*'

I froze but burst into tears.

Sam bent down and picked up the largest pieces of glass. Not moving my feet, I reached for paper towels and started mopping up the counter. When he'd cleared a space, he dumped the glass into my trash can and knelt at my feet, feeling for the tiny, mostly invisible pieces.

'I, I . . .' I couldn't stop crying.

'It's my fault,' he yelled, still mad. At me? At himself? That would make two of us. 'Wait here. I'll get you some shoes. Where are they?'

'My B . . . my Birkenstocks are over by the couch,' I managed to get out.

Sam went to get my shoes while I pulled more paper towels

off the roll. I reached to the sink to turn on the water and wet them. He came back and set the shoes on the floor beside my feet. I saw that he was covered in Coke. I was, too. I could already feel it getting sticky.

It was hard to imagine how that much sticky liquid had come from one glass. We both worked without speaking, Sam on the floor, me on the counter and cabinet fronts, wiping up Coke and bits of glass. I poured the other glass of Coke into the sink, figuring it probably had bits of glass in it, too. Finally, he stood.

'You better wear shoes in here for a while. It went everywhere.'

I nodded and tried to speak. 'I was just . . .'

Sam held his hands up. 'It was my fault. It was all my fault. I'll take this trash out as I go so you won't cut yourself on that.' He sounded disgusted. With me? What had I done? I'd just tried to tell him something, something he ought to be grateful for. He tied the top of the plastic garbage sack and started toward the door.

'Wait a minute!' Now it was my turn to yell. 'Are you just going to leave?'

He stopped but didn't turn around to face me. 'I'm sorry. I'll replace your glass. Just tell me where to find it.'

'I don't *care* about the glass! Don't you even want to know what I found out?'

Then he turned, swung would be more like it, the plastic trash sack barely missing a candlestick on the table beside him.

'Sure! On a Saturday night when I've already had to go back in to work once. When I thought, hey, I'll go see a high school ball game, watch my daughter with her friends, maybe, just maybe enjoy some real conversation. And when that didn't work out, I thought, OK, we'll give this one more try. So, sure! Tell me all about it, because what I *really* want to do on a Saturday night when I'm alone with a beautiful woman is talk about work, *my* work, and how *she* can do my job so much better than *I* can!'

I was stunned. 'I didn't . . . I mean . . . I just . . .'

Sam shook his head. 'Just tell me what the kid said.'

So I told him. I stuck to the facts except to tell him about the boy's genuine fear. He nodded a lot but never put down the trash sack to pull out the little notebook he always carried in his pocket, never made a note.

'OK. Thank you.' He said it, but he didn't sound as if he meant it.

I followed him to the door and watched as he took the trash sack around the corner of the house to the can then got in his car and backed out of my drive. He didn't say another word, but I thought I saw a nod in my direction as he got into the car. Maybe.

Then I slammed the door. I wanted to slam it in his face rather than at his taillights, but it was too late for that. I did what I could. He was too proud to admit that I could find out something he couldn't. Hadn't, anyway. If he didn't want my help, fine.

He thought I was beautiful.

I took a shower to rinse the Coke out of my hair – and so I couldn't hear the phone if he called. I could always check my caller ID later.

While I showered, I thought. How could I find out if Philip Carter had really been at that dinner meeting the night Maureen saw someone in the studio? How could I find out what meeting it had been?

When I got out, I checked my voice mail. No messages. I dripped while I checked caller ID. No calls. OK, if that's the way he wanted to play it. I wouldn't call him either.

But I would call Mark.

FIFTY-FOUR

'Yes, you did catch me in the middle of something,' Mark said. 'It's Saturday night. I have a date. A first date. Even now she's probably wondering why I'm getting calls from other women this late on a Saturday night, and I'm going to have to figure out how much to say. If I explain too much, does that make it seem too big a deal? If I don't explain at all, does that make me seem like it's something to hide? So. What do you want?'

I told him about what Ryan Sanders said Maureen had seen. 'So how could I find out where Philip Carter was that night? If he really was at a dinner?'

Mark groaned. 'Sheesh. Campbell. We've got a police force in this town. They're pretty good. It's not your job. Tell your detective friend. Let him do the work. It's what we pay him for.'

I didn't say anything.

Mark said, 'You don't want to tell him, do you? You're ticked off at him. Or you've made him mad at you.'

'Why are you assuming it's my fault?'

'Ah, hah!'

'I did tell him.'

'OK, so you've done your civic duty. Have a nice weekend.'

'Mark!'

'What?'

'If this were something you cared about, like some minor political corruption, instead of the *murders* of two people, an innocent girl and a *friend* of mine, if you cared about two *children* who don't *know* what happened to their mother, what would you do?'

I seemed to be getting better at alienating people I cared about.

Mark sighed. 'There's a calendar of major events at the *Tennessean*. Charity dinners, political fundraisers, things like that. We can start there. See if there was an event that has an obvious connection to Carter. Then check the guest list. It might pan out. It'll take some time, though, and I'm not going to start before Monday.' He was firm.

'OK.' I was humble. Grateful. 'Thank you.' I let him go back to his date, and I went to bed.

No call from Sam on Sunday. I checked my voicemail and caller ID again when I came home from church. MaryNell called that afternoon, though.

'Julie Davis wants to know if you had a fight with her dad.

He's yelling at her and slamming things around the house, and she can't think of anything she's done wrong – that he knows about.'

Great. I had managed to mess up one more person's weekend.

FIFTY-FIVE

I was determined not to annoy anyone else, so I didn't call Mark first thing Monday morning. I waited. I stopped on the way to work and picked up fresh Krispy Kremes. Hot. The light had been on. I ate one on the way, just checking to make sure they were OK. It melted in my mouth. While Anna, Lee and Martha dug in, I made coffee. At least my work colleagues were happy with me. Until the coffee ran out.

Lunch came and went. I made Anna promise to make Mark hold if he called while I was across the street picking up a sandwich. I hurried, though, and brought it back to eat at my desk.

It was nearly five when Lee turned and said, 'Your friend Mark's on three.'

I grabbed the phone.

'Yeah, OK,' he said. 'There was a Vanderbilt Alumni Association dinner meeting at Opryland Hotel. That's the most likely event. Owen alumni are part of that. I'm working on it.'

I'd wanted to hear more, but that had to be enough for now.

FIFTY-SIX

iss Hale?' The voice on the phone was cultured, familiar, cool and very formal.
'Yes.'

'This is Evelyn Thompson.'

Of course. 'Yes. How are you?'

'I'm fine,' she said, although her tone implied that how she was was no business of mine. 'I want you to know how much all of us appreciate the interest you've taken in Bitsy's . . . disappearance. You've been very . . . persistent.'

'You're welcome.' She was thanking me, wasn't she? I waited.

'This has been very difficult for us. I'm sure you understand that.'

'I know it must have been horrible. How are the children?'

'They're coping. They miss their mother, of course.'

'Of course.'

'I'm calling to ask you, woman to woman, not to involve yourself in our affairs any further. Please. This is a very . . . complicated situation. I'm asking you to understand that. I know you wouldn't want to harm Bitsy further.'

'Harm her further . . .? Now I don't understand. Have you heard from her? Is she alive?' I realized that question was tactless, but she'd taken me by surprise.

'I haven't heard from her directly, no, but . . . Perhaps we made a mistake in contacting the police and the media in the first place. This really is a private family matter. Please. I don't want anyone else hurt.'

'What have you heard? Has Bitsy made some contact?'

Then I heard a different voice. Everett Thompson and the sound of generations of power, money and influence.

'Miss Hale. You've heard my wife. Surely you have enough respect for her distress to honor her wishes? Surely we don't need to involve lawyers? Your . . . meddling is beginning to border on harassment. It's time for you to leave us alone.'

Then the line was dead.

Was that a threat? The last time he'd given me a friendly warning I'd nearly wound up fish bait. Why didn't Everett Thompson want his daughter found? And what was his wife afraid of?

I wished Sam weren't mad at me so I could talk to him about it.

FIFTY-SEVEN

It was Friday before I heard from Mark again.

'It looks like your guy was there, registered at the Owen School of Management table, and filled out a pledge card.' Philip's MBA was from Vanderbilt's Owen School of Management. 'A secretary in the alumni office remembers speaking to him. Told him how sorry she was about Bitsy. Looks like he was telling the truth.'

'Did she say how long it lasted?'

'Dinner, speaker, Blair String Quartet entertained. Three hours or so.'

'OK. Thanks, Mark.'

'Anytime. No, wait. Not anytime. Not ten thirty on a Saturday night. Any Saturday night!'

'How was I to know you'd have a date?' There, I'd done it again. Said the wrong thing to one more person. 'I didn't mean . . . I mean, how was I to know you'd have a date right then?' It was no use. He was still laughing when I hung up.

Clouds hung low as I drove home. The wind was warm, from the south, but it was damp, heavy with rain waiting to fall. If I had the Spider today, I'd have been tempted to put the roof down, daring the clouds, smell the Gulf air. But the Spider was still at AAAAuto, and I was still in a leased Camry. All I could do was put the window down and open the moon roof.

Who would have been poking around in Bitsy's studio?

And what was he doing?

I puttered around the house all evening, hoping Sam would call to say he was sorry. The phone never rang.

About eleven, I thought of one more question for Mark. It was Friday, not Saturday, but I decided I could wait until the next morning. I was trying hard.

'Mark?'

'Yeah. What time is it?'

'It's eight o'clock. If you're not up now, you should be. My grandmother would have said you're sleeping your life away.'

'Did your grandmother work for a morning newspaper?'

'Listen, how many people were at that dinner? And did they have assigned seating?'

'What? What are you talking about?'

'Was it huge? Philip Carter. We know he was there, but did he stay?'

There was silence. 'Yeah. Yeah. It was in the Presidential Ballroom. It holds a thousand. I'll check. They might have had assigned tables. I'll get back to you.'

I was absolutely sure my watch had stopped more than once that day. I picked up the phone and punched in all but the last digit of Sam's number twice, but I hung up. I hadn't yelled at him. Let him call and apologize.

MaryNell called to see if I wanted to go with her to Melissa's basketball game that night, but I told her I had too much to do. I just didn't say what.

I ran out of things to wash, dust and clean before the phone rang.

'Campbell?' It was Mark.

'Hey! Hi! Did you find out anything?'

'Yeah. Maybe. People bought tables, so you were assigned to a certain table. Philip was at a table that the company bought. His brokerage. He was there, signed in, came to the table and talked with everybody there, filled out his pledge card, handed it to the table chairman. Then he told them a fraternity brother was there that he hadn't seen in ten years, said he was going to sit at that table for dinner and he'd see the rest of them at work on Monday.'

'So he could have come home and done it.'

'Done what? Gone into his own studio?'

'I don't know what. Yet. But somebody went in there and did something and didn't want to be seen doing it.'

'Yeah. Maybe. But there's more to the story. Some of the people from his brokerage, the people he'd been supposed to sit with, saw him on the steps when they were waiting for their cars at valet parking. They went to a club for drinks. So he was with them until midnight.'

'But in between? He had time?'

'Well, there were at least two and a half hours when he was unaccounted for. We're going to do some more checking, verify the bar story.'

'I knew it! Thanks, Mark.'

'And I found out all this on a Saturday. You really owe me.'

'I do. You're a genius,' I said.

'Now what?' he asked.

'What do you mean?'

'I mean, what are you going to do next? You going to tell your boyfriend the policeman or you going to do something stupid?'

'Is there a none of the above? I don't think he's my boyfriend. I'm not sure he's speaking to me now.'

'Did you call him on a Saturday night and interrupt the first real date he'd had in who knows how long?'

'Something like that. Will you all be telling the police?'

'Probably. That way they can do some of the legwork. Let me know what you're doing, OK? Be careful, don't do anything dangerous?'

'I'm always careful.' I hung up on his snort.

I had to find a way to get inside that studio and look around. I spent the rest of the afternoon trying to figure out how. I called Philip Carter about four. He was friendly, but I thought he sounded a little impatient.

'Thanks for calling, but I don't guess we know anything new,' he said.

'I was hoping we could get together and talk about things, what I found in Mexico, which wasn't much . . . Can I buy you dinner, coffee?'

His tone was wary. 'Uh, no. I'd like to do that, but I can't tonight. I have plans. Dinner with some clients. Maybe one night soon, though.'

'Sure. Look, I'm sorry I bothered you.'

'Not at all. We'll stay in touch.'

That was stupid, but at least I knew he wouldn't be home tonight. I wouldn't sit home waiting for Sam to call tonight.

FIFTY-EIGHT

I changed into dark pants, sweater and jacket, and waited for dark. I didn't want to wait too long and give Philip time to get through with his meeting and come home. At seven forty-five I blocked caller ID from my phone and called to make sure Philip Carter wasn't home.

No answer. That didn't prove anything, but so far, so good. I could try again with my cell phone when I got closer.

I found a dark stocking cap to cover my blonde hair. I had seen *To Catch a Thief*; I knew the uniform. I grabbed gloves, a penlight flashlight, set my cell phone on silent and left. Clouds were gathering. Good. No moonlight.

From the car, I called Sam's house. I thought I should leave word where I was going, but I didn't want him to try to stop me. I hoped no one would be home. It was Saturday, and Julie had a basketball game. Maybe Sam would be going to the game, too. No one answered the phone, but I left a message. That way, nobody could stop me, but someone would know where I'd gone. If I didn't make it back. When Sam heard the message he'd be mad, but if I found anything, I'd have to tell him, and he'd be mad anyway.

'Sam, this is Campbell. Saturday night, about a quarter to eight. I've gone to check out Bitsy Carter's studio. Don't worry. I'll call you later.'

I exited off I-65 South at Harding Place and tried Philip's phone again. No answer. Across Franklin Road, across Granny White, across Hillsboro Road. When I was a couple of blocks from Bitsy and Philip's house, I tried one more time. Still no answer. I drove up their street. No visible lights, but their house was set back in trees. I went past, turned around and drove back by. Nothing. At the bottom of the street, I turned around and went back. I went past their drive again, turned around, and parked on the street a hundred yards uphill. I sat for a minute. No alarms, no startled dogs. Normal outdoor sounds. OK.

I got out and walked quickly back toward the Carters' drive. Just before the driveway pavement I ducked into the trees to the side of the drive. I followed the winding drive so I wouldn't get lost in the dark. I stayed about twenty feet to the left of it. The house was dark; no security lights on. I passed the spot where Philip had been burning trash the day I had come by. The white ash circle stood out in the darkness. Wind whipped dried leaves and ash into a swirl around my head. Rain was coming. I could smell the moisture in the air.

I kept my distance from the house as I approached the studio. I still hadn't seen any sign of life, no car in the drive. The children were staying with their grandparents, and Philip had said he'd be away. I pulled out my cell phone and hit the redial button. I could hear the faint ringing inside the house, but nothing else except the wind rustling dead leaves in the trees.

I crouched down when I got to the studio, feeling silly since there was no one around, and duck-walked to the entrance. Large clay pots stood on either side of the door. I tilted the one nearest me and felt underneath. Nothing. Well, dirt, maybe a slug. Yeech! No key. I slipped quickly to the other side and tilted the other pot. I slid my hand underneath and felt the key just as I heard the faint sound of the metal sliding against concrete. I closed my hand over it, pulled it out and set the pot back down silently.

Now. What about an alarm? I hadn't thought about an alarm. Oh, well, no one was here. If an alarm went off, surely I could get to my car before police got here. Unless it was a silent alarm, wired directly to the police.

I was committed to it. I wasn't going to give up now. Not when everything was going so well. I wouldn't want to call Sam to bail me out with the Belle Meade police, but I would if I had to. OK.

Still crouched to the side of the door, I reached up, inserted the key, and felt it turn, smoothly and silently. The door opened without a squeak, and I blessed Bitsy for regular maintenance and liberal use of WD-40. I slipped inside and closed the door behind me. Apparently, the studio wasn't alarmed.

Inside, I stood and stretched the muscles in my legs, already threatening to cramp from crouching. I listened. Nothing. In a room with windows, there is never total darkness. Here there were lots of windows and a skylight, and even without a moon there was enough light that I could pick out the shiny metal kiln in the gloom. I made my way to it carefully. The last thing I needed to do was knock a stool over into a table and have jars crashing to the floor.

I knelt behind a counter and listened again. Nothing but the wind. I decided I could risk the flashlight. Sheltering the light with my body, I played the tiny light around the floor in front of the kiln and the door to the kiln itself. Nothing. Some dust maybe. There was usually a film of clay dust. I started to touch it then remembered my gloves. Feeling like a kid playing some spy game in the neighbor's back yard, I put on a glove and swiped a small path through the dust on the kiln. The kiln was cool. It certainly hadn't been used recently. I slowly, quietly unlatched the door and opened it.

I don't know what I expected to see. A last piece of Bitsy's clay work, forgotten in the kiln? Something horrible, a grinning skull on the rack inside? There was nothing. Putting my body between the kiln and the front windows, I turned on the penlight again and peered inside. Dust. Or ash. Bitsy would never have left ash in here. If a piece were left in too long, at too high a temperature, would it crumble like this? I felt inside. Ashes. And a few irregular lumps. I pulled one out and felt with my ungloved hand. It didn't feel like pottery, but I wasn't sure how it should feel if it had been left like this. I stuck it in my pocket. Whatever Maureen had seen someone putting in the kiln was incinerated now. And I couldn't see anything here that helped.

Time to go home.

I carefully closed and latched the kiln door and quietly made my way back to the entrance. I opened the door and stood for a moment, listening. Outside, everything was dark and still. I slipped outside, closed and locked the door. I knelt to put the key back in its place. Now the breaking and entering was through.

I retraced my path, staying in the tree line and using the driveway and ash circle as landmarks. I was beginning to feel raindrops. In the distance there was lightning. I made it to the street. There was my car, on the side of the road, facing downhill and away from the cul-de-sac at the end of the street for a fast getaway. Don't tell me television is an intellectual wasteland. It's an education.

I stood in the shadows for a few seconds, watching and listening. Nothing, except that it was beginning to rain.

I walked up the street quickly, opened the door and slipped inside, closing the door behind me.

Several things hit my brain at the same time. Relief, I'd made it. More relief, the car interior lights hadn't come on to give me away. The interior lights hadn't come on. Why? And . . . someone was in the car with me.

FIFTY-NINE

The electronic lock button snapped, and Philip Carter said, 'Thanks for dropping by, Campbell.'

Philip was in dark clothes, too. He must have watched the same TV shows. But his gun gleamed darkly, and it was pointed straight at me.

Of course, if Maureen Kennedy had seen someone snooping around the house, sneaking, if not breaking, into Bitsy's studio while Philip was away, the one person she would have gone to was Philip Carter. And if Philip hadn't been away, if he had snuck back at a time when he'd given himself an alibi, if he were afraid of how much she had seen, afraid that she might talk to someone else, talking to Philip Carter would have been a mistake. Maybe a fatal mistake.

I didn't have to worry about saying the wrong thing. I couldn't speak.

I forced myself to breathe.

'Find what you were looking for?' he asked.

'No. I didn't find anything. I mean, uh, I wasn't looking for anything, umh, so I don't know what I didn't find.' My voice trailed off. 'I was just looking around . . . Yeah.'

'I wish you hadn't. I really wish you'd just . . . found a hobby and left us alone.'

He sounded so reasonable. Right at that moment, I was wishing I'd done just that.

'Well,' he continued, 'I guess let's drive.'

Would he shoot me? Would he shoot me here on the street outside his house? If I just unlocked the door and rolled out. I couldn't run and escape him here before he could shoot me, but would he? Maybe. If only someone would come by, walk a dog, need cigarettes from the store. Why didn't people smoke anymore?

'OK. Where?'

'Let's just drive. I'll tell you where to turn.'

My cell phone was in my left hand, out of sight. I turned it on. Could I dial 911 without looking? I felt the nine and pressed. I started the car.

'Both hands on the wheel, please.'

I let go of the phone, laying it in the molded pocket on the inside of the door beside me. The rain was steady now. I turned on the wipers, put the car in drive, and released the parking brake. Then, with both hands on the wheel, I drove. Slowly. Downhill. Clean getaway.

'I haven't had time to plan this, you know. Park or lake? The Warner Parks would tie you to this side of town. I think lake. A mishap at the lake. Everybody's going to think you should have known better. A young woman alone. They'll be right.'

I could hear my parents – and Sam. At least this bought me some time. If only I could make a call. How could I keep him from noticing that I had taken my hand off the wheel? I had to start talking, distract him. I supposed it was too late to pretend that he and I didn't both know that I knew he was the murderer.

'I don't understand,' I began. I took my right hand off the wheel, just gesturing, nothing threatening. At the bottom of the street, I stopped. 'Which way?'

Philip took a deep breath. 'Left. You don't understand? Should I care?'

Gone was good, old, friendly Philip. I put my right hand

back on the wheel, turned, let my left hand slide off. I found
the phone, found what I thought must be the one button and
pressed twice. I had to put my hand back on the wheel. At
the next intersection I turned right. Maybe in the busy traffic
in Green Hills I might be able to do something. I might even
find a policeman.

'Bitsy never left town, did she?'

Philip laughed.

'Mexico? The woman on the fishing boat wasn't Bitsy. Who
was she?'

Philip laughed again. 'I hoped your little trip to Mexico
would keep you busy. You and the detective. I thought you
could both have a little fun, take your minds off Bitsy. Nice,
romantic place like that.'

'Who was the woman?'

'Friend of Mick's. Somebody he knows up in Tijuana. It
doesn't matter.'

'Mick? Captain Mikwozhewski?' I felt for the send button.

'Both hands on the wheel, please. Wouldn't want your door
to come open. Accidents happen that way, you know.'

'The same kind of accident Maureen Kennedy had?'

'That would be tough to prove.'

At the Harding Place–Hillsboro Road intersection, I stopped
again, pulling into the left lane to turn toward Green Hills.
The streets were slick now with rain.

'But why? Why kill your children's au pair?' I took both
hands off the wheel, gesturing again. I put the right one back
on, dropping the left. I felt for the send button and pressed it.
I hoped. I'd been hearing about technology that would track
cell phone call locations. Would the 911 operator use it? I
couldn't remember. What would happen when the dispatcher
answered my call? Would she assume the call was a mistake,
someone pressing a programmed call button without knowing
it? If I were calling from a landline phone, I thought she'd
see the address. But a cell phone number? Would she listen?
Would she track it?

'But what about you and Bitsy? You killed Bitsy, didn't
you?' If it was too late to pretend ignorance with Philip,
maybe I could say something that would catch the dispatcher's

attention. There had been so much on the news about Bitsy's disappearance. Would she hear Bitsy's name and make the connection?

SIXTY

'What do you think?'

I took a deep breath. 'I think you killed Bitsy. I think you somehow left your car at a hotel near the airport. I think you took Bitsy's car out there, left it in long-term parking and took a shuttle, maybe a taxi, back to the hotel where your car was. I think you got someone, I guess the woman from Tijuana, to fly to Ixtapa under Bitsy's name and go fishing. I don't know about Maureen Kennedy. I don't know if Mr Thompson is mixed up in this somehow, but I don't think Maureen died because she hit her head when she fell off a horse.'

Philip laughed again. 'Everett Thompson. All-powerful, all-knowing Everett Thompson. With the spine of an amoeba and just about as much intelligence. No. Everett needed that money as much as I did, more maybe, but he didn't know how to do anything but bully Bitsy. But he was good – and experienced – at being a bully.'

Traffic was light coming into Green Hills. Late Saturday night is not its busiest time. And not a policeman in sight. 'What money?'

'Bitsy's money. All tied up.'

'So why did you have to kill her?'

No answer.

'She was leaving you, wasn't she?'

'Bitsy? The perfect wife?' Philip's voice was heavy with sarcasm. 'The perfect mother? Pure, innocent Bitsy, everybody's favorite, with a lover?'

'If she left you, you couldn't get to the money. But I thought Mr Thompson controlled the money.'

'He managed the trust, but only until Bitsy turned thirty-five. Next month. Then she'd have control.'

'So why hadn't he reported her missing?'

Philip laughed. 'I convinced him she left town because she was upset with him. He'd been trying to get her to agree to back up some investments with the trust money. He was giving her time to cool off.' Philip laughed again, and it wasn't a pretty sound.

'Where is Bitsy?'

Philip didn't answer.

'This won't work, you know.'

Still no answer.

'I left a message. With the police. Saying I was going to your house.'

'I'm not sure I believe you, Campbell.'

'It's true.' One more traffic light, and I would be past the Green Hills retail district heading into town. He'd probably tell me to turn onto I-440 to head toward Percy Priest Lake. My chances were running out. 'I left a message on the detective's voicemail. It's the kind of thing that would make him mad. He's probably got an APB out on me already. I'm the last person you want to be in a car with.'

'Things seem pretty peaceful so far.'

'So where is Bitsy?' Nothing. Up ahead at the next traffic light I thought I saw a police car on the cross street. Suddenly, horribly I thought, surely he couldn't have . . .? 'The kiln? No!' I felt sick. 'The kiln?'

The light was red, and there were no other cars at the intersection besides the police car. This was it. I floored the accelerator, blasting through the intersection just as the police car began to pull into it. Philip was thrown back. I hoped he had the safety on that revolver.

'What are you doing?' he screamed.

The police siren screamed, too, and blue lights started flashing.

'Keep going,' he yelled. 'Stop and I'll shoot you.'

I had to do something to keep his aim off, at least. I spun the car, turning at least a hundred eighty degrees on the wet street into the opposite lane. Philip was thrown sideways, and the gun went off. So much for the safety. The windshield was a spider web of splintered glass, and I couldn't see anything but a kaleidoscope of blue light.

I punched the seat belt button, flipped the lock and opened the door. The car was still moving, momentum carrying it as it slid sideways. I jumped, rolled, fell out of the car as Philip fired again. I hit the asphalt, and seconds later the car hit a utility pole and wrapped itself around it. How was I going to explain this to the leasing company? I couldn't hear anything except the police siren.

Then a police officer was running toward me.

'Stay calm, ma'am. Keep your hands where I can see them. You OK?'

'Please. The man in the car. Philip Carter. He's got a gun. He's a killer. Sam Davis. Call Detective Sam Davis.'

'You stay right here.'

In the distance I could hear more sirens. I wiped liquid from my eyes – rain? blood? – looked at the car and saw Philip trying to climb out.

The police officer was yelling, 'Drop the gun!'

I closed my eyes.

SIXTY-ONE

When I opened my eyes a paramedic was leaning over me. That seemed to be happening too often recently. 'I'm fine,' I said. I was trying to sit up. I was not going to a hospital. I did not have a concussion. I knew what that felt like; this wasn't it. I knew where I was. I knew what was going on. And I knew it was only going to get worse when Sam got here.

'Yeah,' he laughed. 'I think you are, except for this blood. Just lie there though. Have you had a tetanus booster lately?'

'I'm OK. Really. Where's Philip Carter?'

'He the guy in the car? I don't think he's going anywhere.'

The rain was cold, and there did seem to be blood all over me, but nothing felt broken. The paramedic shined lights in my eyes, told me to squeeze his hands. There were crowds of people around and more arriving every minute: police, a fire

engine, paramedics. Radios squawked. I had not helped
Hillsboro Road traffic.

'Where were you when I needed you?' I mumbled.

'Ma'am? Did you say something?' He was cleaning scrapes
and cuts on most every exposed part of my body. Blood was
seeping through from a few unexposed parts, too.

Suddenly Sam loomed over me. 'You are *never* driving
my car!' he said forcefully. 'Is she OK?' he spoke to the
paramedic.

'Yeah, she's fine. Cuts and contusions. She's lucky.'

Sam looked at the gauze squares the paramedic was using
to clean my wounds. 'Make it sting!' he barked as he turned
and walked away into the rain.

SIXTY-TWO

A patrolman drove me home. He said he would wait
in the drive until Detective Davis got there. Great.
I had time to take a shower and change into flannel
pants and a fleece pullover, clothes that weren't shredded
and soaked, but it wasn't long enough. I dreaded what Sam
would have to say. Too soon, there was a knock at the door.
Lights were flashing. More patrol cars were outside
when I opened the door to see Sam and another detective.
Frank.

'Hi.' I spoke to Frank. He was the only one not glaring at me.

'Ma'am.' He nodded.

'I made coffee.' Sam's acknowledging nod was more of a
jerk. 'I'll just go get it now,' I offered.

'No!' Sam barked. 'Detective.' He spoke to Frank. 'Get her
statement.' Sam went to the kitchen.

Frank looked apologetic. 'I need to ask you some questions,
ma'am.'

I nodded and sat on the sofa. Frank sat across from me.

'I'll just record this if you don't mind, ma'am.' He laid a
small tape recorder on the coffee table.

'Does it matter?'

'Ma'am?'

'Nothing. OK. Go ahead.'

It was a long story, and there was a lot of frustrated eye-rolling when Sam got back in the room with the coffee. I told them about Ryan Sanders' story and the dinner at Opryland, and Sam made a phone call. I didn't think Ryan was going to get a lot of sleep tonight either. When I got to the part about the kiln, I got up.

'Where do you think you're going?' Sam demanded.

'There's something you might need to see. I'll be right back.'

'Well, don't try going out a window. I've told the guys outside to shoot you on sight.'

I thought I heard a stifled snicker from Frank.

I came back with my gloves and mutilated black slacks.

'The kiln was full of ashes. I think there are some on my gloves.'

'We need an evidence bag here, Frank.'

'I think they're Bitsy's ashes,' I said, 'and this . . .' I turned the slacks' pocket inside out to show the hard, white lump without having to touch it. 'I think you might want to test it, too.'

'I'll call CSI,' Frank said quickly and reached for his cell phone.

Philip had been caught on the airport security cameras entering the terminal just after the time recorded on the parking receipt for Bitsy's car and leaving a few moments later by cab. Security cameras at a business-centered hotel a mile away showed him entering and leaving the parking lot. The times were consistent with our theory. Sam was on his way to pick him up when a dispatcher had called him about a weird call she had received. She had been about to disconnect when she thought she overheard Philip's name and Bitsy's and thought it was worth calling Sam. Then he heard about a crazy woman wrecking a white Camry in Green Hills, and he knew it was me.

The police had also found the link between Philip and Mick Mikwozhewski. College roommates. Judges were losing sleep that Saturday night, too, what with arrest warrants, search warrants, extradition requests.·

Everett Thompson had acknowledged that Philip had been at the farm on the day Maureen died. Philip had been in Everett's office when Maureen and the children arrived. When Everett came back after seeing them off on their ride, Philip was gone. And Everett admitted that he had believed that his daughter had left home to escape his trying to force her to assign part of her trust as repayment of his debt.

A crime scene unit was at the Carter home. Besides analyzing the contents of the kiln and the circle of ashes near the drive, police investigators were already tearing out the slate tile and retrofitted antique fixtures in the Carters' newly remodeled master bath.

A crime scene investigator arrived and sealed my gloves and slacks in evidence bags. He tested my hands for residue of the ashes.

The whole time Sam was yelling.

'You nearly got yourself killed. Worse, you've screwed up our evidence. Tim!' he yelled at the crime scene investigator. 'Tell her that she's screwed up our evidence.' Tim looked at me sympathetically. 'Never mind. It won't do any good.' Sam turned to me. 'She never learns!'

I sat there, answered everyone's questions, and tried not to cry or look like I was cowering. I still had some pride.

Later, after everyone else had left, Frank deciding to catch a ride with the crime scene investigators, Sam was still fuming. 'Do I have to follow you around every minute? I take my eyes off you and . . .'

Words failed him. Finally. And he left.

SIXTY-THREE

t rained for days. I spent a lot of the next week downtown at the police station. I told everything I knew to different detectives over and over. I saw a lot of half-hidden smiles, especially when Sam was anywhere nearby. Not that he spoke to me unless he had to. I gradually realized that I had really embarrassed him professionally. I couldn't undo that.

I saw myself on television, rain-soaked, bruised and bloody the night of the wreck, then trying to rush past the cameras on my way into the Criminal Justice Center later. Neither was a good look. I decided I needed to lose twenty pounds, but it didn't matter because I was going to have to move to an uninhabited island without cable TV anyway.

MaryNell came and brought sympathy. Sam's daughter Julie sent cookies by MaryNell's daughter Melissa. Secretly. Melissa said Julie was afraid her dad would kill her if he found out. She said he never stayed mad very long, but then she'd never seen him like this before.

More details emerged. Some were in the newspaper; I picked up others on my many visits downtown. I answered the same questions over and over again.

Philip had apparently killed Bitsy in the bathroom off their bedroom. He'd killed her in the tub and washed her blood down the drain. He'd wrapped the body in an old blanket and hidden it for a couple of days until the remodelers had torn out enough trash to justify a fire. One evening, after the workmen left for the day, Philip had pulled two-by-fours and trash lumber out of the construction crew's dumpster and burned Bitsy's body with the remodeling trash. He'd fed the fire and burned it until nothing was left but her bones. And then he had snuck home when witnesses would say they had seen him at the Opryland Hotel to put the bones in the kiln in Bitsy's studio.

All the while Dan Neal had been overseeing that bath's renovation, which Philip was counting on to get rid of DNA evidence, Bitsy's body was wrapped in a blanket and hidden in the woods nearby.

He'd left home one evening dressed for the alumni dinner and had taken a change of clothes. He had come back, filled the kiln, and slipped away to change and return as expected.

He'd had weeks to cover his trail.

Then, when the new bath was done, he told the workmen to stop, not to go on with remodeling the other rooms until Bitsy returned home.

The CSI investigators found bloodstains under the new tile. They found bits of bone in the kiln, just as you find bits of bone in cremated remains. They were searching through the Rutherford County landfill where the dumpster had been emptied, looking for debris from the Carters' house. It would take a few weeks for DNA results, but Evelyn Thompson finally knew where her daughter was. And she was trying to figure out how to explain that to her grandchildren.

Investigators also found mud on a pair of Philip Carter's shoes that seemed to match that in a wooded area of the Thompsons' Maury County farm. By itself, that wouldn't have been enough to convict him, but close to the spot where Maureen had fallen, they found a large tree limb that looked like it might prove to have fibers from clothes Everett Thompson could testify Philip had been wearing the day Maureen Kennedy died. If they were really lucky, the long, reddish hairs on it might prove to be Maureen's.

It wasn't easy; it wasn't Perry Mason, but the police were patiently building a case that would put the murderer of two women in prison for a long, long time.

The Thompsons had a private memorial service for Bitsy. I didn't feel they'd want me there. I didn't know if Dan Neal went, but I knew what he would be thinking. None of this could bring her back.

Sam didn't call.

Finally, more than a week after my wild ride with Philip, Agnes Elliston called. 'Buck up!' she said. 'Anybody would think this whole mess was your fault. Why aren't you at work? I need a travel agent. And you need to quit moping. I'll see you tomorrow morning at nine.'

I went back to work and made it through the day. And the next.

SIXTY-FOUR

It was a Saturday morning a few weeks later. The rain was gone; the sun was out; and the wind was from the south. Sea air from the Gulf. I decided it was time to visit my Spider.

Charlie was there, of course. AAAAuto is open until noon on Saturdays.

'Miz Hale! Come on back. We was just about through paintin'. She'll be good as new before you know it.' Behind Charlie's computer office was the real clean room. Air purifiers ran in there whenever it wasn't in use, pulling all the dust from the air. When the room was in use, it was to paint cars with the precision and care that Charlie put into everything else. I looked through a window built into an interior wall to see the Spider, windows and trim covered with brown paper and masking tape, in a fog of red.

'Here's a bench,' Charlie said as he pulled it up. 'Have a seat.' I sat down and watched as the masked man inside the clean room made the last sweeps with his paint sprayer. He finished, and the steady thumping of the air compressor stopped. The red fog began to settle on and around the Spider and the painter, the red just one more layer of paint on the floor.

Charlie came back and explained the work that remained to be done. Not much. I'd have the Spider back in less than two weeks. Most of that time would be needed for the paint to dry and cure. Charlie was proud of the work and with good reason. 'She's comin' back real good, Miz Hale. That's a good car.'

The Spider had been a mess when she had been towed in last fall. The insurance company called her a total loss. And now she was almost ready to drive again. Bitsy would have understood. I didn't have to be anywhere, so I just sat.

I'm not sure how long I had sat there when I heard Sam's voice. 'I thought I might find you here.'

I didn't turn around. 'You really are a hotshot detective.'

'Ah, well,' he admitted, 'it wasn't the first place I looked.' He sat down beside me. 'The car looks good, real good.'

I nodded. 'Yeah.'

'What are you doing?' he asked.

'Watching paint dry.' One tear spilled from my left eye.

Sam put one arm around me and wiped the tear away with the other hand. Before I knew it I was sobbing into his fleece pullover. It was the first time I'd cried for Bitsy.

'I'm sorry, Campbell. I always hate this mess, but I'm really sorry because she was your friend.' I kept crying, and Sam just held me. Finally, Charlie came back.

'Miz Hale. I'm sorry, but it's time to lock up. The Spider will be OK here. She just needs some time to dry good and cure out. A few little things. You'll be drivin' 'er out of here in no time. It'll be all right.'

I nodded and wiped my face. Charlie went back to the front of the shop.

'I look awful when I cry,' I said.

'Yeah,' Sam agreed, 'but you clean up good.' He pulled a handkerchief from a pocket. 'There's a baseball game this afternoon.'

I sniffed.

'It's been too long since we've seen a ball game.'

'Yeah?'

'There'll be hot dogs,' Sam promised.

'Give me a minute.' With the cold water in Charlie's rest room, Sam's handkerchief, and a spare mascara I keep in my purse, I cleaned up a little. Sam was talking to Charlie when I came out. Sam smiled and nodded.

'I'll give you a call, Miz Hale, tell you when she's ready.' Charlie locked up behind us as we walked out to our cars.

'Meet you there?' I asked.

Sam grinned. 'I'll be right behind you.'

ACKNOWLEDGMENTS

Thank you to David for your continuing encouragement, to Brandon for catching the ball, to Julia for the cookie recipe, to Hank and Margaret for the original owner's manual, to Kathy Carman for the TBI tour, to Debbie Pitts for the education in pottery, and to Howard, retired Navy and the best neighbor in the world.